Beautiful Agony

MUSIC CITY DIARIES

KRIS BUTLER

Beautiful Agony

MUSIC CITY DIARIES

KRIS BUTLER

Contents

Blurb

Motorcycles, burly men, and danger were all part of my childhood. Growing up in the Maverick's—Mississippi's biggest and toughest motorcycle club—was different than most of the girls at school, but I loved every minute of it. So much, that my goal was to join the ranks when I was of age.

When I passed Maverick Culling Defense, my dad's program to become a Maverick, I thought my life was finally beginning. Turned out, being a twenty-year-old virgin was the least of my worries.

When my life took a massive shift in a direction I never saw coming, I was left with a brokenness that consumed me. Could I turn this utter agony around into something beautiful? Or was I destined to always be that broken girl, afraid of her shadow?

Foreword

This book is connected to the Tattooed Hearts series. This book is a prequel, featuring Darcie. If you haven't read Riddled Deceit or Smudged Lines, there might be some small spoilers, but it won't take away your experience reading them. This is just the beginning of Darcie's story and how she became the Darcie we know and love from Lennox's story. It does end on a cliffhanger.

This book has sexual scenes meant for adults. It is a reverse harem romance, meaning that the main character won't have to choose. This book also contains explicit language.

This book has content warnings for sexual assault, rape, and self harm. If these topics are sensitive for you, please read with care. My hope is that I've provided a safe place to explore those issues and have treated them with respect, along with my characters. Always take care of yourself first, lovely reader.

To finding beauty in the brokenness.

One

DARCIE

anting, I stopped for a second, needing to catch my breath. I'd always thought I was in shape, but apparently, 'run a moderate timed 5K' in shape and 'run for your life' in shape were two different things. Go figure.

A snap had me jumping, and I took off running again, cursing the leopard print boots that had looked amazing earlier with my outfit.

"Stupid cute boots; why couldn't you be more functional?" I hissed under my breath as I came out of the trees I'd been trampling through. I'd hoped it'd be a good enough diversion, but it had only slowed me down as much as the person chasing me.

When I finally made it to the street, I sagged in relief, hoping to blend in with the crowd of tourists. It was Friday night, and a festival was going on.

People littered the streets, giving me excellent coverage as I weaved in and out of them. Glancing over my shoulder, I didn't see my pursuer anymore, and I smiled in relief.

Turning down a familiar street, I picked up my pace, needing to only make it a few more blocks, and I'd be home free. My heart raced, my skin covered in a layer of sweat in the summer heat. I didn't dare look at my make-up, already feeling the eyeliner and mascara sweating down my face. My hair was damp on the back of my neck and felt lifeless as it hung there. I desperately yearned for a shower, but I knew this would be worth it in the end. I was so close.

With throbbing feet, I stomped up the stairs, the lethargy sinking in with each step I took. That had been a close one. Pulling out the keys, I unlocked the door and stepped into the place that had become a second home to me.

My father sat in his chair, his legs spread wide as he regarded me. His long beard hid most of his face, and the rest was obscured by the hand placed there, covering his mouth as he watched me.

I stood, waiting to hear what he'd say. The monitors blinked behind him, the buzz from the servers a soothing sound. Shuffling on my feet, the tiredness in my limbs and the need to wash the stink off got the better of me, and I folded.

"Well? Did I pass?" I asked, biting my lip.

The door opened behind me, my pursuer entering to stand next to me. He knocked into my shoulder, and I smiled, taking the encouragement for what it was.

My dad stood, walking toward me. Hank Preston was an intimidating man. He had to be in order to control the Mississippi Mavericks—the motorcycle club he was President of. For most people, motorcycles were either a hobby or a nuisance; for us and others, they were a way of life.

They were everything.

Hank gripped my arms, pulling me forward. "You were almost caught, but you were able to outsmart him in the end. I thought you were done for when I saw what you were wearing today." He gave me a disapproving look, but I shrugged, smiling.

"Sometimes sacrifices have to be made for cute footwear." I beamed at him, pleased he wasn't yelling. My dad grunted, the corners of his mouth lifting a smidge.

"Well, Mad Dog, what do you think?" my dad asked, using the road name of the man next to me. "Do we have another graduate of the MCD program?"

I looked at the guard next to me, the man as familiar to me as my dad. He'd been around most of my life in some fashion, either visiting with his family, or when he'd come to go through the program himself. He was only a few years older than me and had become the son my father never had. Mad Dog peered down at me with his dark blue eyes, assessing me. Despite being close, I knew he'd never go easy on me. Neither of them would risk it for my pride.

It wasn't a matter of passing, but life and death.

If they didn't believe me to be ready, then I'd go back through like I had three times before. But this time, it felt right. This time, I'd felt strong and in control.

"I think she's ready, Pres," he finally said. My shoulders relaxed, and I breathed out, a huge smile spreading across my face. My dad pulled me into a hug, holding me tight.

"I'm so proud of you, peanut." When he held me close, I knew it was my father—the softy—speaking, and not the hardass Pres. "I thought I was done for when your mother gave me a girl, but you've shown me how strong a woman can be in this world. I still worry about you, but that's a father's right. I don't want to let you go, but at least now, I know you can handle yourself." He kissed the side of my head, and I pretended not to feel the wetness that dripped down his face.

Turning to Maddox, I wrapped my arms around him as well, needing his approval. "Promise you didn't go easy on me?" I whispered so only he could hear.

"Promise. You're too precious for that." He squeezed me tight, pulling back a little. "Now, go shower. You stink, Runt."

Sticking out my tongue, I giggled as I skipped off to the shower. I didn't care that he called me that today or told me I smelled. The only thing that mattered was I'd officially passed the MCD program. I was a Maverick.

"What are you going to do now?" Chelsie asked. She was a family friend I'd grown up with, but we hadn't ever been close. We didn't have much in common outside of our ages and our dads being in MCs. My dad had always told me to be friendly, though, needing to build relationships between clubs. She wasn't bad, just kind of boring. Her older brother was a lot more interesting, but he didn't always join her when they visited. Which was a shame, since he was hot as fuck.

She'd arrived two days ago with her mother and father, and I was already bored, ready for them to leave. I tended to be more active than this, needing to do something other than lounging out by the pool. But here we were, day two of laying out as the pool glistened in the sunlight, beckoning us in, but Chelsie didn't want to get her hair wet, so gossip and tanning had become my routine.

Kill me now.

With school ending a week ago, I didn't even have that to escape to. It felt nice to officially be a college graduate. I'd just finished two years at the Community College getting an Associate's degree in business management. It wasn't what I wanted to do, but I figured I could use it with the club. My only goal for my future had been to be an MCD graduate, and I'd finally done that.

Covering my eyes, I glanced over at her, remembering she'd asked a question.

"Not sure. Ride, I guess. You still going to the University of Tennessee?"

"Yep. I can't wait to get out of Alabama and away from all of the Rebels crap." She grimaced, looking over at me, remembering I didn't hate MC life as much as she did. I waved her off, not caring what she thought; to each their own.

"What are you studying again?" I asked, fighting a yawn.

She opened her mouth to answer when a body

zoomed by, cannonballing into the pool, a large splash spraying us. Chelsie screamed, cursing out the offender. All the while, I laughed, the cool water feeling nice on my warm skin.

The body emerged from the water, and I sucked in a breath, sure I'd fallen asleep and was fantasizing. Chase, Chelsie's older brother, lifted himself out of the water like a commercial model. The water beaded and rolled off his skin hypnotically. He sat on the ledge, flipping his hair back, smoothing it out of his face, and I swear it was all in slow motion. When he turned, my insides quivered, and I had to remind myself to breathe.

He was too fucking good-looking. Chase had an air of danger, and there was something about him that called to me. It was probably destructive as fuck, but I was twenty, so what did I care? Living in an MC, you'd think I'd get all the dangerous urges out of me. But here was the thing. When you were a princess in an MC, no one touched you, no one looked at you, and they most definitely didn't harbor any illicit thoughts about you. Nada.

It wasn't any better at school. Without it even having to be said, everyone knew not to try. That, or no guy was brave enough to face my father when they picked me up.

Basically, I was twenty, a virgin, and horny as hell.

And prime cut man candy was directly in front of me. So what if he was the son of my father's rival? They were friendly, a truce having been called years ago. In fact, they were here now to talk about a bigger alliance. It was the first one my father was going to let me in on now that I'd passed.

"Chase! You're such an ass," Chelsie chided, glaring at him.

He looked over at me, winking. I almost swallowed my tongue, my cheeks heating at the gesture. He'd never looked at me that way before, but as his eyes bore into me, scanning my body, I didn't know what to do.

Was it because I was a graduate now? Or was it just the bikini? Should I push my breasts out more? Arch my back? Wink back? Flirt? Shit! How did one flirt? I take it back. I was so not prepared to date.

As the litany of things ran through my head, Chase and Chelsie had gotten into one of their epic arguments, allowing me to calm down and center myself.

"Quit being such a little bitch. You don't own people. I can flirt with whoever I want."

"Oh, is that what you're doing? Every time there's a girl around me, you hit on them. I can't bring friends over because you always end up fucking them, breaking their hearts, and then I'm one friend less because 'my brother sucks,'" she screamed.

"Actually, they usually do the sucking." He laughed, dodging her hand. She'd gotten up to swat at him at some point, and I watched the two go back and forth. It was a good reminder. I couldn't let myself get distracted by a cute smile. I wanted to show my father I could be part of the club, which meant not being distracted by dick.

Chelsie walked over, towering over my chair. "Just so you know. He fucked like three girls before we came here. I wouldn't be surprised if his dick fell off. I wouldn't touch him with a 10ft pole if I were you, but I can see on your face you don't care. So, just use protection and don't hate me when he breaks your heart." She turned, the silk robe she'd worn to the pool flying out behind her in her haste. "And this is why I can't fucking wait to head to Tennessee," she muttered before slamming the door to the house.

Turning back, I found Chase staring at me, nothing but lust in his eyes. He sat down on my lounge chair, trailing a finger up my leg.

"Don't listen to her. She's just jealous that her friends only talk to her to get to me."

The comment made me bristle, and I wondered if I'd been under the cute guy spell myself. Clearing my throat, I moved my leg, pulling both up to my chest, and wrapped my arms around my legs.

"Well, maybe you should expand your fuck pool to exclude her friends."

He moved forward, eating up the space I'd just created. Leaning close, he whispered in my ear as his fingers trailed over my arm. "It sounds so erotic when you say fuck. Hank's lil' girl is all grown up now. I wonder what else has changed."

He skated his nose against my neck, causing goosebumps to break out. My head warred with my body as it wanted to give into him, accepting what he had to offer.

"Chase, you're needed inside," Maddox said, his voice stern. We jumped apart, and I avoided looking over at him. Chase sighed, leaning his head down. His hand still gripped my ankle, his thumb brushing against the top of it.

"Yes, Sir Cockblock."

Maddox growled, but didn't retort, waiting for him to let go of me and leave.

"This isn't over, babe. We'll continue this conversation later." He stood, walking off, and I kept my eyes fixed on the water. My breathing was heavy, and I didn't know how I felt. Was I embarrassed I'd been caught? Had I wanted him to touch me? I thought I had, but maybe that was the fantasy and not reality.

A shadow loomed over me, and I looked up, meeting familiar dark blue eyes. "You okay, Runt?" I nodded, not able to find the words. His jaw tensed as he held eye contact, a storm brewing within.

"Don't tell my father, please." I finally managed to say. "This deal is important to him."

"What don't you want him to know? Was that not consensual?" he asked, his tone changing as he stepped forward. His fist unclenched and re-clenched as he stared at me.

"Just let it go, okay? I'm fine."

I stood, picked up my pool cover-up, and placed it over my head. I ignored how close we stood and how good his skin felt when I brushed my arm against his. I ignored how better it felt compared to Chase. I most definitely ignored the way his eyes zeroed in on my chest or how he seemed to suck in a breath as I brushed past.

Yeah, I was good at ignoring things.

Too bad things weren't good at ignoring me.

Diary #1

Dear Mom,

Chase finally arrived today, and he flirted with me. It was weird because it was something I'd wanted for so long, but it didn't feel the way I thought it would when it happened.

Maybe it's just because I'm not used to it? Boys paying attention to me? I kept waiting for the punchline.

In the end, Maddox interrupted, and I was both grateful and angry he did. At times, he infuriates me, and I wish he'd butt out of things. I'm not a little girl anymore. In fact, being a graduate of MCD means I can take care of myself.

I wish you were here. I miss you every day.
Darcie

Two

DARCIE

The food I'd been playing with slid off my fork, and I wondered how long I'd have to sit through this dinner. It wasn't that I didn't enjoy being part of the business side of things now, but if I had to listen to Stanley "Agonizer" Driscoll talk about how great he was at golf for another minute, I was likely to explode. We were an MC, not a country club! At least he was staying true to his name. I was definitely in agony.

Looking around the room, I took in the bored looks of my father's most trusted men and felt somewhat relieved. Their bearded and sun-worn faces were just as bored as mine. I was starting to wonder what type of club the Diamonds were. Based on this steak dinner with actual napkins, I was getting the picture that it was a lot fancier than ours.

I met Tiny's eyes as I scanned the room, holding in a laugh as he rolled his. He mimed Agonizer droning on, and I couldn't stop myself from letting the sound slip that time.

"Something you'd like to share?" Agonizer asked, the room turning to look at me. I met my father's stare and swallowed; the disappointment reflected there was hard to take.

"Sorry, sir. I just remembered a joke." He sat back, scanning me. I watched as his eyes lit up as he took in my curves. I hadn't worn anything scandalous tonight, but the way his eyes drifted over my breasts, you'd think I was sitting here topless. I didn't like the way it made me feel, and my father's insistence on waiting until I was thirty to have sex didn't sound so bad right then.

Okay, maybe that was stretching it, but if men looked at me like Agonizer was, then I didn't want anything to do with it. I'd happily remain a virgin at this rate.

"I'd like to hear it." He smirked, calling my bluff.

I gulped, looking over at my father. His eyes were hard, jaw clenched tight, and I looked for some confirmation this was what he wanted me to do. He gave an imperceptible nod, and I glanced back at the man I was beginning to fear. He hadn't been like this before toward me, but apparently, acquiring boobs meant I had a neon sign for every perv to try their hand.

"What do you call a cow with no legs?" I asked, my voice barely above a whisper. It didn't matter because it was so quiet in the room, someone could've heard it a room over.

"What?" he asked, smiling, his eyes filled with something I couldn't identify.

"Um, ground beef."

No one laughed, waiting to see how they should behave from the Agonizer. When had he gained so much power? It was like looking at a different man. Before, I'd always thought he and my father were equal. He reigned over the Alabama clubs and my father, the Mississippi. Based on his clothes, his attitude, and the way everyone deferred to him right now, I had to assume that had changed.

My father was no longer the scariest man in the room, and for some reason, that terrified me the most.

After a quiet few seconds, he let out a loud, boisterous laugh, slapping the table and causing me to jump as the dishes clattered. He pointed at me, smiling, though I didn't believe it was natural for one second.

"You're funny." The smile dropped off and he sat forward. "That's gonna have to go when you come to my club. We like our women meek and silent." His eyes changed, turning to slits as he stared at me, and I struggled to put words together.

His place. Meek. Silent. His place.

"I'm sorry, what do you mean *your* place? Am I going for a visit I didn't know about?" I glanced from him to my father, not liking what I saw there. A resigned look covered my dad's face, and when I met his eyes, it was the first time in my life he dropped them, refusing to look at me.

Swallowing, I glanced at the other men around me, and their faces looked like mine. Filled with shock, fear, and confusion. So this wasn't common knowledge.

Immediately, my mind flipped over to my training, and I started to categorize the information I knew to form a plan.

A deal was being brokered.

My dad didn't seem to have power here; in fact, it seemed like he owed Agonizer something.

I was going to their compound.

Chase was suddenly all over me.

I was twenty and a virgin.

Fuck. Fuck. Fuck. No, this couldn't be possible. My father would never allow it.

I glanced at him again, pleading for him to look at me, to acknowledge the pain and anxiety I was feeling. Anything! But he stared at his plate as the Agonizer droned on, talking to no one but himself.

"Daddy?" I whispered, the sound perceptibly weak even to my own ears. He flinched but didn't look up, cutting his steak into small pieces.

"Nothing to fear, little one. I promised to take good care of you. I'll get you nice and broken in before I hand you over to my son." He smiled lasciviously, and my whole body shivered. I'd rather cut off my arm than have that man touch me anywhere. That was going to be a hard pass from me.

"Thank you for the offer, but I'm going to have to decline." A gasp rang out from Chelsie, but I ignored it. I couldn't look at her, worried she'd known and hadn't told me. I scooted my chair back, needing to be far away from here.

"Darcie, stop," my father said, halting me. I kept my back to him, unable to watch him say the words.

In front of me stood Maddox, his ripped jeans and dusty boots such a familiar sight. His face was stone as he stared over my head, disgust and ill-intention brimming in his eyes. When my father started to speak, he dropped his eyes to me, and I held onto them like an anchor.

I couldn't do this. I couldn't hear my father say he'd traded me. It would break me. So instead, I focused on Maddox's dark blue eyes, falling into them and letting him wrap me up in his protective-ness. He'd always been there, so I let him take this too.

I hated myself a little that I wasn't strong enough to face my father, but I wasn't, and it was better to know your strengths and weaknesses instead of blindly failing.

When a hand touched my elbow, I jumped until I realized it was Maddox. "Come on, Runt, I'm to help you pack." The words were gritted out, but not toward me. If anything, it was the softest he'd ever spoken to me.

Numbly, I nodded, letting him lead me. We walked to my room in silence, no words needing to be shared. When I got to my door, I couldn't open it, knowing what stood on the other side.

"I can't do it, Maddox. I can't." My lip quivered, and I braved looking up at him. To my surprise, he didn't judge me for falling apart. If anything, he seemed to want to comfort me. His hand lifted in the air, stopped halfway between us. He glanced down at it, noticing the grease and oil, and dropped it.

"You can, Runt. You're ready."

Sucking in a breath, I wiped my eyes, taking a moment to gather myself. Opening my door, I quietly walked over to my bed and pulled out a duffle bag. I placed it on top and opened it, and stared at the empty space. I'd dreamed of packing up and moving somewhere one day but never like this. This club had been my home, these rowdy men my family. To leave with that monster felt wrong.

"Why is this happening?" I asked, sitting down on the bed.

"I don't know. Your father's been having meetings without me lately. I think something happened. Something big. It's the only thing I can think of for this choice. Your father loves you, Darce."

The shortened name warmed me inside, but I pushed it away, not wanting to feel anything other than the cold numbness at this moment. If I let myself feel, I'd break into a million pieces, never to be put back together. I couldn't afford that right now.

"Will it hurt?" I blurted, not having planned to ask my pseudo brother about sex.

He grimaced, only briefly looking at me. "I'd like to lie and say no, but it will be even worse than normal, knowing him. I'm sorry, Darcie. I wish I had more power, and I'd... I dunno, but I'd do something."

"I think if there was another solution, then my father would've already found it." The words sounded hollow, but I knew they were true. I didn't doubt my father's love for me outside of this moment. So, I had to trust there was a purpose.

Together, Maddox and I managed to pack two duffles and a backpack of my things. I placed my mother's journal, a music box, and a small photo album in the bag, wanting them closest to me while we rode. The other things were just clothes and replaceable, but these, I wanted to keep safe.

When it was done, Maddox patted my shoulder, standing to leave. I felt like I needed to say something since it might be my last chance.

"Maddox," I said, stopping him at the door.

"Yeah?" he turned, looking at me.

I swallowed, the words wanting to stay buried, but I urged myself to say them, knowing I had nothing else to lose. "I always thought it would be you, the one my father gave his blessing to. Thank you for watching over me all these years. You've been a real friend to me. I'll miss you the most."

His body tensed, and I watched as he wrestled with something. Eventually, he nodded, clearing his throat. "I'll miss you, too." With those words, he turned and walked out the door, taking a piece of my heart I hadn't realized belonged to him.

Laying down on the bed, I curled my legs up, and the tears fell, knowing that whatever lay ahead of me wouldn't be easy.

My door opened with a bang, and I jumped. My legs were stiff, my muscles sore from the position I'd fallen asleep in. I blinked, wiping the sleep from my eyes as I tried to figure out what had caused the sound. A moment later, a body fell on top of me, their weight heavy, and I tensed, trying to push them off. Whiskey breath met my face, and I turned, screwing up my nose as I tried to find fresh air and get away.

"Your father thinks he can go back on a deal? Well, I'll show him. Once I'm done with you, he won't be able to do anything with you. Then you'll be mine at half the cost."

Agonizer ranted, and I tried to piece together what he said. Hope surged up when I realized my father wasn't sending me away. He'd changed his mind!

The massive frame of Agonizer was impossible to move, and as he fumbled with his belt buckle and zipper, I knew what was coming. I pushed and clawed at him, trying to wriggle free, but his whole weight lay on top of me.

"Stop moving, you little bitch."

He sat up, and I took the opportunity to buck up, attempting to throw him off me. His meaty hand came down, pinning my hands above my head, locking them into place. Not giving up, I wriggled and shifted, attempting to use some motion to knock him over. I hadn't waited all this time for some drunk asshole to take my virginity from me because he felt owed. No way in hell.

It was no use, though; the man weighed close to 250 lbs and was mostly muscle, despite his age. He freed his dick from his pants, and I squeezed my eyes shut, not wanting to see it. I heard him chuckle before reaching down to yank off the shorts I'd been wearing.

"You think you're so fine. Walking around in those booty shorts and you don't expect men to fuck you? I'll make you a good sweet butt, show you how to please a real Pres."

His words were jumbled together, and I tuned them out, giving in to what was happening at this point. I was tired of fighting and wondered if I just grinned and beared it, if it would be over quicker. Surely, that was the better option at this point? I couldn't think, my brain going to a safe place.

Squeezing my eyes shut tighter, I willed away what was happening. If I pretended it was a dream, maybe it would be.

He pushed in, and pain like none other ripped through me, and I screamed, no longer able to hold it back. His hand clamped over my mouth, muffling the sound as he pumped into me. The fight returned, and I thrashed against him. Now that he was holding my mouth, my arms were free, and he attempted to grab one. I smacked and hit, clawed and bucked, not willing to let him have it easy now.

Thankfully, the scream had been enough, and the door slammed against the wall, something splintering. I heard a smacking sound in the next second, and the body was removed from me. A blanket was tossed over me, and I curled it around me, my body shaking now that the fight was over. Tears rolled down my face, and I felt someone smoothing my hair, whispering to me.

"I'm so sorry, peanut, I'm so sorry. Please, forgive me. I'm an idiot. I'm so sorry." Over and over, he repeated himself, holding me to him as he rocked me. After a while, my body stopped shaking, and I let my father comfort me.

"Tank, we need to go. If we have any chance of leaving, it's now. Tank!"

I opened my eyes, finding Maddox staring at my father as he sobbed into my hair. "Okay, you're right," my dad said, pulling back.

He looked into my eyes, struggling to find the words. "Go with Maddox. He'll keep you safe. I'm so sorry, peanut. I never meant for this to happen." He pulled a sweatshirt over my head and handed me a thick envelope, closing my hand around it. "This will get you guys on your feet. I wrote everything down that you need. You can never return to Mississippi, Darcie. Do you understand?"

"Never?" I asked, the words not making sense.

"No. This is the last time I can see you or contact you. From this point forward, you'll be a ghost. I'm sorry this had to happen. I didn't mean for it to end this way. I hope you'll find it in your heart to forgive me someday."

"Tank, we need to go."

My dad sucked in a breath and leaned forward, kissing me on the forehead. "Listen to Mad Dog; he'll take care of you. Go."

I nodded, somehow managing to get off the bed. I avoided looking at the man knocked out on the floor. I avoided looking anywhere but right in front of me. A backpack was placed over my arms, and the hood was pulled up on the hoodie. Maddox peered down, pushing my hair into the hood.

"You with me, Runt? Just a few steps, and we're home free, okay?"

I nodded, trusting him to get me somewhere safe. It used to be this club, but that was no longer accurate.

He took my hand, the callouses a comfort I needed, grounding me enough to make my legs move. I didn't look back, I didn't say goodbye to my father, and I didn't look at the man who'd just raped me. I couldn't. Keeping the hood up, I focused only on the two steps in front of me.

Two steps.

Then two more.

Then two more.

Before long, we were outside, and I felt a weight lift off me. Maddox pulled me toward his bike, and I followed.

It was the snap of a twig that had me startling, jumping to the side as Chase stepped out of the shadows.

"And just where are you two headed? You wouldn't be running away with my bride-to-be, would you, Mad Dog?"

"Chase," I croaked. At the sound, he looked down at me, taking me in. His eyes drifted over my whole frame, and I saw the moment he realized something wasn't right. He dropped the cocky guy act, stepping forward in concern.

"Darcie, what happened? Are you okay?" It was the boy of my childhood, the one who played house and baked cookies with me when his sister wouldn't. I hadn't seen that side of Chase in years.

"Your father's what happened," Maddox growled, stepping in front of me.

"My father? Wait, what?" Chase kept trying to peer around the brute in front of me to see me.

I touched Maddox's arm, stepping around. "Yes, your father, he um," I said, my lip starting to tremble. "He came to visit me."

Thankfully, it was all I needed to say as I saw understanding flash across his face.

"Shit. I'm so sorry, Darcie. He hasn't been the same the past year. I don't know what's changed, but something big is coming. I…" He scrubbed the back of his head, pulling at his dark locks as he debated. "Here." He reached into his pocket, pulling out money, a phone, and a business card. "It's not much, but hopefully, it will help. Call me when it's safe. It's untraceable."

"Like fucking hell will I do that," Maddox said, stepping back in front of me. "You need to turn and go inside now before I decide to punch you out cold like dear old dad."

"Listen, shit for brains, I don't care what happens to you, but I do her. I wasn't on board with this whole marriage thing, but I didn't want her to be raped by my father either. No one deserves that. So, I want to help. I care about her enough to not want my father to have his clutches in her. You don't have to like me, but know that."

Chase breathed heavily, and I heard the sincerity in his voice. I reached out, taking the items he offered. "Thank you, Chase." Stepping forward, I kissed his cheek and then walked over to Maddox's bike. He stood staring at Chase, probably debating punching him, but eventually turned and placed our stuff in his saddlebags. He straddled the bike, revving his engine, and turned, waiting for me.

I stepped forward, the thought of spreading my legs uncomfortable, but I knew I needed to do it to get out of there. Sucking in a breath, I straddled the bike, holding onto him tight, pressing my face into his back as I winced at the pain. Clinging to him, I cried into his back as we drove off, leaving the only home I'd ever known behind.

Diary # 2

Dear Mom,
    I can't.
    Darcie

Three

MADDOX

I drove into the night, speeding as much as tangible without killing us. The wind whipped against my face, doing nothing to cool the anger firing through my veins.

Everything I'd done today had been wrong.

Tank had been acting funny, but I let it go, not questioning him, trusting the man I respected above none other. That creep Chase had been sniffing around Darcie, but I let him go instead of punching him. I almost kissed the most perfect girl, but I stopped myself, duty and honor coursing through me, letting her go.

And look where honor had gotten me.

After a shot of tequila, I'd gone to fix the one thing I'd let go of, deciding it was time to kiss my princess and show her just how much she meant to me. I wasn't going to let her go with Agonizer.

But I was too late, and that asshole had stolen something precious from her.

Rage had filled me when I heard her screams, and I thundered into her room, ready to kill anyone who dared touch her. Darcie was mine, even if she didn't know it yet.

From the moment I kissed her under the willow tree when we were kids, she always had been. She probably didn't even remember it, but that had been it for me. And every summer when we visited, I fell more and more in love with her until I finally was able to enter the program at eighteen, leaving my father behind.

She thought none of the guys wanted her because of who her father was, but it was because of me. I threatened any of the boys at school who tried to lay a hand on her. After a few punches, they fell in line. It had been Hank who stepped in, stopping me from telling her my feelings back then.

"She has to prove she can make it on her own in a club before you can claim her. If not, no one will respect her. Do you understand? She has to show the others she's rightfully their queen and didn't get the position because

*of me or you. Darcie wouldn't want it that way either.
You know this."*

It had made sense at the time, and I vowed to help her with the program. If she passed, no one could deny her place in our world.

Hank had started the program when he became Pres, wanting the men in his club to be more than motorcycle hotheads looking for pussy and a good time. If they passed, then they got their patch. It wasn't about killing or scoring drugs in the Mavericks, but respect. If you could hold your own and pass one of the most grueling tests around, then you belonged in the Mavericks.

I'd learned about the program when I was fourteen and I wanted nothing more than to go through it right then, but my father made me wait. He had his own club to run, after all, and it wouldn't look good for his son to leave his. So, I bargained that checking it out would be a good learning opportunity, while not mentioning I never intended to return to his.

Hank had fashioned the Maverick Culling Defense after his time in the Marines, using the Bootcamp structure to test prospects on their fitness, ingenuity, and survival skills. It was a testament to their character if they could pass.

The Mavericks looked like your typical motorcycle club from the outside. They rode bikes, wore leathers, and were covered in tattoos. They drank, fucked sweet butts, and bent the law at times. We weren't saints, not by a long shot, but there was something more to being a Maverick. Partially, it was due to the fact our operation wasn't about guns, drugs, or sex, instead making the program a valuable part of initiation.

More men and women failed out the first week than made it through. Which was why the fact Darcie had finally passed was a big deal. She'd earned her spot amongst our ranks.

So, why had Hank sold her to Agonizer? It didn't make sense. It went against everything we stood for, and I wasn't going to let it go.

When Tank had come into her room, finding me standing over the asshole, he barely managed to get me off of him before I killed the scumbag.

"Stop! You can't kill him, Maddox."

"Like fuck I can't!"

"There's more at play, son. I want you to take Darcie away from here. Go, pack a bag. I'll explain everything."

It was those words that had me dropping the asshole and heading to my room, tossing a few things in it before I headed back. I didn't need much outside of Darcie and my bike. She'd been my main reason for joining, so without her, it didn't make much sense to stay, anyway. I'd come with two purposes, and at least one of them would come to fruition.

Her arms tightened around me, and I felt her body tremble behind me. The reassurance she was with me as the miles disappeared between us and the compound was the only thing that quelled the fire raging in me.

I'd driven for two hours when I decided it was safe enough to stop. I turned into a town and found a convenience store still open and pulled in. The bike clicked as I turned it off, and sound, outside of the wind and the engine, returned to my ears. Placing my hand on top of hers, I linked my fingers in one and stepped off the bike. I couldn't let go just yet. Everything I wanted balanced on a precipice, and I didn't want it to tip over in the wrong direction.

"Runt, do you want to go inside?" she blinked, looking up at me. Her pale blue eyes were shadowed, and I didn't like it. "I'll go with you if you want. I need to fill up, and then we'll be back on the road. I want to put more miles between us before we stop."

She nodded numbly, letting me pull her into the store. When the ding on the door sounded, she jumped, burrowing into my side. Wrapping my arm around her, I walked with her to the bathroom, glad it was the unisex one. Locking the door, I grimaced when I saw the state of the place. But it would have to do.

Taking her in, I looked her over, assessing all of her injuries. Taking a wet paper towel, I gently placed it against her lip. She winced but let me dab it to wipe the dried blood.

"Hold that there. I'm going to take off the hoodie so I can see more. Are you okay with that?" She looked up, her eyes vacant, but nodded. Gently, I took each arm out of the sleeves and pulled the neck to lift it over her head. Placing it on the sink, I took her in. There were some cuts and scrapes along her arms; red marks and bruises were already forming.

"You fought hard, Princess."

Her shirt was torn, and I wished I'd thought to bring in a new one for her. It would have to wait. Bracing myself, I bent at the knees to inspect lower. Blood had trailed down her leg, and I swore. Standing up, I grabbed another paper towel and wetted it. As softly as possible, I trailed it up her leg to remove the evidence of Agonizer's greed. She tensed when the wetness touched her leg, her body trembling more as a whimper left her lip.

"I'm sorry, Princess. I'll be quick."

Once she was clean, I placed the hoodie back over her and helped her wash her hands.

"Do you need to go to the bathroom?" I asked, clearing my throat.

She looked up, almost like she was trying to decipher my words. Finally, she shook her head, wrapping her arms around herself. Pulling up the hood again, I pulled her into my side and exited. At this time of night, thankfully, there weren't a lot of patrons to avoid being seen by.

Heading to an aisle, I grabbed a first-aid kit, a bottle of water, and a pack of Starburst. The clerk looked at us suspiciously, but he dropped his eyes when he saw my patch, scanning the items I'd placed on the counter.

"You okay, miss?" he asked, building up the nerve. "This man bothering you?"

"I'm good," Darcie said, curling into my side more.

I narrowed my eyes at the man but nodded in respect. "You know who I am and still asked that?"

"No one should disrespect a woman, not even a Maverick."

"That took balls." I scratched my jaw, taking him in. "Just so you know, I didn't. I'm the one rescuing her. I respect your willingness to stick your neck out for my girl, though. If you ever need anything, let

Tank know Mad Dog owes you a favor." He swallowed, nodding. "Twenty on pump 3. Take care, sir." I tapped the counter, leaving more cash than necessary, and took the bag, leaving the man in shock.

Favors of the Mavericks were a big thing. Even if I was a ghost from here on out, I knew Tank would honor my request. It might seem risky, but I hoped it also helped him keep his mouth shut if anyone else came by asking. Kindness and honor got you further than fear most of the time. I learned that from Hank, the opposite of my father.

When we got back out to the pump, I started it before opening the saddlebag. I searched through and pulled out a pair of soft pants for her.

"Here." She looked at them like a foreign object, so I helped her step into them, pulling them up. "Do you want to keep your backpack on or put it in here?" She stared, and I worried she was going into shock.

"Darcie!"

She blinked, looking up. "I'll keep it."

Nodding, I smoothed her hair and pulled her into a hug. I'd never get tired of holding her. The click of the pump had me pulling away, kissing her forehead. Putting the gas pump back, I locked the saddlebags and climbed back on my bike. This time, I handed her the helmet I'd grabbed out, able to think more clearly when it didn't feel like our lives depended on it.

Like a pro, she hooked it on and climbed onto the back of the bike, wrapping her arms around me. She seemed a little more cognizant this time, and I hoped she was coming out of her fog some. I didn't want to have to worry about her falling off the back of the bike.

"Just a few hours more, Princess."

I felt her nod into my back, and I started the engine, setting off, praying we'd make it.

A few hours later, I pulled into a motel parking lot, exhaustion forcing me to call it quits. Dawn was starting to break, but I couldn't go any further without sleep.

"I'll be right back. Will you be okay by yourself?" I asked as I stepped off the bike.

Darcie nodded, pulling her arms around herself. She looked around at the parking lot, but it was mostly vacant with no one out at the moment. She seemed to ease the further from Jackson we got. Turning, I didn't linger, knowing it was better to get inside the room as quickly as possible. Using a fake name, I reserved the room for two days despite not planning to use it that long. A trick I'd learn in the MCD program.

Paying cash, the clerk slipped the key across the counter, and I pocketed it, turning to leave. I needed to be forgettable, which was hard at 6'5". At least my arms, which were covered in full sleeves, were covered, but I'd need to do something with the leather jacket soon. Too many people knew who the Mavericks were, and that was something no one would forget in Mississippi.

Darcie wasn't on the bike when I stepped out, and I cursed under my breath. My heart started to pound in my chest as I searched the area for her. Looking behind cars, I ducked around a large van, checking in backseats and under them one by one.

"Hey," she said, the sound the most beautiful in the world. I stopped and turned, finding her standing on the curb, a bag of chips and soda in her hand. "I got breakfast." She smiled, but it didn't reach her eyes, and I knew it was an attempt to make herself appear better, rather than really wanting to smile.

Clasping my chest, I hung my head, taking a few breaths. "For Pete's sake, Darce. You about gave me a heart attack."

She snorted, a genuine smile breaking free for half

a second. "Sorry. I got hungry." She raised her shoulder. "Room ready?"

"Yeah." I walked over to the bike, grabbed our things, and walked her around to our room number. Opening it up, I stopped her before she walked in. She rolled her eyes but stopped, stepping back.

"I highly doubt someone is waiting for us, but by all means." She gestured with her hands, opening the bag of chips. She took a loud bite, the sound ricocheting around us, and I narrowed my eyes at her.

"Really?" She shrugged, continuing to eat her damn chips. Huffing, I quickly walked through the room and made sure it was clear. I sat our bags down on the dresser and pulled out the first aid kit. Stepping into the bathroom, I turned on the light and inspected the shower. It was decent with a tub and appeared clean.

"Hey, Princess, do you want to take a shower or bath?"

She peeked in, eyeing the tub. "Yeah, I guess a bath would be good. Um, do you think we could stop by the pharmacy later?" she asked, dropping her eyes.

"Sure. What do you need?" I turned on the tap, fiddling with the temperature as it started to fill.

"Um, the morning-after pill," she whispered.

The rage I'd managed to lose built up in me

again, and I clenched my hands against the side of the tub. "Yeah, Princess. I can do that for you."

"Thanks, Maddox." She hugged me around the waist when I stood.

"I'll do anything for you," I whispered into her hair but wasn't sure if she heard me over the sound of the water. Pulling away, I set a towel down on the toilet and stepped out. "Just let me know if you need anything else."

"Wait!" she shouted, some of her fear returning. "Um, do you think you could stay in here with me? I just don't want to be alone yet. The memories flood me more when I am." She bit her lip, her hard-won confidence earlier leaving as shame took root.

"Absolutely, but you'll be, um, you know." My cheeks heated.

"Don't tell me boobs scare the big badass Mad Dog. Which is a stupid road name. I always wanted to tell you that," she quipped, the shaking slowing in her body. She reached down to turn off the water, and I closed my eyes, not wanting to check her out in this state.

"I'm not scared of boobs," I gritted out. "And you have told me every day since I was given Mad Dog that it's dumb." I reminded her, squeezing my eyes closed.

"Oh, yeah. That's right." I heard some of her

brightness returning and decided if it was at my expense, then I'd deal with it.

"What would be a better road name for me? Not that it matters. I'm no longer in a club." I didn't mean to sound sad about it. I'd gladly run away with her any day, but the Mavericks had been my family, and I was sad to leave them behind.

"I'm sorry about that," she said as she slipped under the water. "Fuck." I heard her suck in a breath as she lowered herself more, but I kept still, not wanting to violate her any more than she'd already been today. I heard the curtain close, and I peeked out, seeing she'd pulled it. "There. It's now Maddox-decency appropriate." She giggled, lighting my heart on fire.

"You laugh, but you know your father would kill me if he found out."

"Yeah," she said, and I wish I could take back mentioning her dad. Sitting down on the floor, I spread my legs out the length of the tub. "I think your name should've been something to do with shadows or stealth."

"Oh? Why's that?" I asked, shifting myself. Now was not the time to get hard, dick. Get it together.

"You've always been my shadow; it just seems fitting. Though, you're full of light when you choose to show it, so maybe not. I'll think about it and rename you. We can make our own club."

I smiled, liking the sound of that. "The Darcie and Maddox club, huh?"

"Sounds perfect to me."

It was quiet after that, the only sound was the water shifting at times. I laid my head back against the wall, the warmth of the room lulling me to sleep.

"What do you think my father's letter says?" she whispered.

I jerked, realizing she'd asked a question. "I don't know. He's been cagey these past few weeks. Something was going on he hadn't told me about."

"I'm nervous to read it. What if I don't like what it says, and it changes who my father is to me?"

"Avoiding hard things doesn't make them untrue, Princess."

It was quiet again for a moment, but she voiced the question I'd been wanting. "Why do you call me that?" she asked, her voice soft again.

"Because you are. You're my princess." She sucked in a breath, pulling the curtain back, her face peeking out.

"What does that mean? Because I think I know what it means, but I don't know if that's just me wanting it to mean that. So, explain."

Our faces were close, and I knew this wasn't the

right time, but the man who'd been in love with her didn't care. Cupping her jaw, I peered into her eyes, looking for any sign of hesitancy. I couldn't show her everything, but I could show her this.

Placing my lips on hers, I held them there, not wanting to push too far. I wasn't an idiot, but I didn't want to miss another moment with her. Pulling back, I held her gaze, searching for any sign she wasn't okay.

"Does that clear it up for you?"

She nodded, her eyes tracking mine. "I... I..."

I placed my finger over her lips. "I'm not expecting anything. I know that what occurred tonight won't go away with the bathwater, but I'm here. I've been waiting for years already; longer isn't going to kill me. I just couldn't go any longer without you knowing. I didn't want to waste another opportunity. You don't know how much I'm already beating myself up for not kissing you earlier." I paused, grinding my teeth. "Maybe if I had, then this wouldn't have happened." I clenched my jaw, looking away. I couldn't look into her eyes and see the truth of that statement.

This was my fault. I'd been a coward and let him walk in and scar her.

"Hey." She patted my cheek, pulling my eyes to her. "The only one to blame is Agonizer. No matter the actions any of us took, it wouldn't have stopped him. I," she shook her head, "I don't blame you. I'm mad at my father, but I know deep down he's not responsible either. Let's just get through this and figure out the rest later."

I caressed her check. "Deal. You're starting to turn into a prune. Let's get you out of that water. I need some sleep before we can ride some more."

"Okay."

Standing, I missed her touch immediately, but I knew what I'd said was true. Holding out the towel, I waited until she took it, the water draining as she pulled the curtain back.

"I'll be right outside the door. I'll grab your bag."

She nodded, but I didn't miss how she moved forward where she could see me. Quickly, I grabbed the duffle off the dresser and handed it to her. She closed the door, leaving it open a crack, and I took the opportunity to change.

Sliding off the leather jacket, I knew it was the last time I could wear it. I'd worked hard to earn it, but it wouldn't mean anything in the life ahead of us. Folding it, I placed it in the bottom of the bag and pulled out a clean shirt and boxers. I left my socks on because hotel floors creeped me out and pulled off the comforters, leaving only the sheets and blankets on the beds. When I was fixing the pillows, she stepped out, a t-shirt covering her body.

I didn't want to stare, but now that I'd admitted my feelings, it seemed my body thought it had free rein to show them. She smiled sheepishly, walking over to climb into the bed and pulling the covers up tight under her chin. Sliding into the opposite one, I turned off the lights, turning to face her.

"Night, Princess."

"Night, Maddox."

The AC unit kicked on, rattling against the wall as we both stared at one another. My eyelids started to close when her voice broke through the quiet.

"Can you sleep with me?"

"What?" I asked, sitting up. "Um, I don't think that would be a good idea."

"No," she said, and I wondered if she was blushing as she hid her face. "I mean actually sleep. I don't think I can be alone right now."

"Oh, sure." I pulled the blanket off and got out of my bed and slid into hers, staying on top of the covers. Pulling my sheet around me, I laid there, staring at the ceiling. Now that I was this close to her, my body was fully awake. Thankfully, her breathing started to even, and she fell asleep, her breaths pulling me under as well.

Her whimpers woke me a few times throughout

the next couple of hours, and it made me vow not to let that asshole survive if I ever saw him again. Fuck the law. No one harmed her and got to live. She was right. We'd make our own club, and *that* would be our first rule.

Assholes didn't deserve to live. Starting with Stanley "Agonizer" Driscoll.

Diary #3

Dear Mom,

Everything hurts.

My heart. My soul. My body.

I don't even know how to handle this much pain. It's all-consuming.

Every sound, I hear his grunts.

Every movement, I see him over me.

Every touch, I feel his hands on me.

I can't erase him.

I'm so sick of seeing and hearing him. I wish I could rip out my eyes and ears, but the memory would still play across my mind.

Not even sleep makes it go away, if anything, it's more vivid there.

I'm hanging on by a thread. My mind is a dark place.

The only bright spot is Maddox.

But I worry that soon, I'll darken him, too.

I just want it to stop. Make it stop, please.

Love,

Darcie

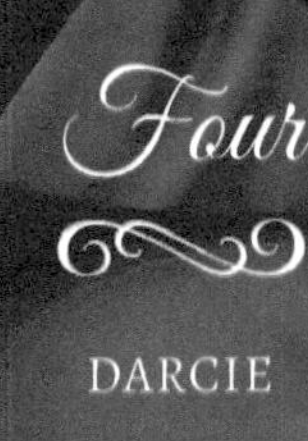

Four

DARCIE

It took me two days before I was ready to read the letter, and even then, it was more about making sure we had all the information to proceed, not that I was prepared to face whatever my father had to say.

I was pretty confident at this point that without Maddox, I would've taken my own life. I wasn't as strong as he kept telling me. I'd smile and nod when he said beautiful words to me, but I felt anything but beautiful.

It was complete and utter agony.

Agonizer had been named aptly as he'd brought nothing but pain to my life.

I wanted to escape it. Dangerously dark thoughts circled my brain, and I contemplated what it would feel like to do them.

But then I'd see Maddox's dark blue eyes, reminding me of the depths of the sea, and I'd calm, finding solace there.

I needed him so damn much, it terrified me.

We bounced around a few places and he'd come through with the pill. It had been uncomfortable riding around on the bike as my ovaries decided to turn themselves inside out. If sex led to that, I wasn't sure if I wanted it. I never wished to be a virgin again so hard in my life.

Sitting on another motel bed, I held the thick envelope in my hand. The paper was heavy, and he'd used his nice fountain pen. A tiny smudge on the letter E was the only blemish against the stark whiteness.

"Are you sure? I could read it for you if you'd like?" Maddox asked. He was sitting in front of me, gently grasping my ankle. His thumb moved back and forth in a carefree gesture against my skin, sending tiny shivers through me. His face was solemn, and he watched me with an intensity I was still getting used to.

"I think I need to. Everything feels out of control, and nothing makes sense. I think I need to read it with my own eyes for it to sink in."

"Okay. I'm here if you need me." He squeezed my foot, relaxing the tension I had.

"Thanks, Maddox. I can never repay you for the kindness you've shown me."

"You never have to; that's the beauty of it." He stopped, biting his tongue, and I wondered what else he wanted to say but held back. Dropping my eyes, I looked at the handwriting one last time before I flipped it over, opening the back.

Inside I found papers folded together, a picture, and a key. Setting the key and photo aside, I unfurled the papers, smoothing them out on the bed. Sucking in a deep breath, I picked it up and started reading.

Peanut,

Life doesn't always make sense, and as I find myself writing this to you, it's because of that statement.

I've failed you, and for that, I owe you an explanation.

I wasn't always a good man, and some would say I'm still not one. But I tried to take the things I'd learned, the life I lived, and make it better for the next generation. As you know, the Mavericks haven't always been what we are today. I hadn't planned on running an MC, much less changing one overnight, but when I returned from my stint in the Marines, I knew I needed something.

Making the MCD program gave me a way to make us better and provide a purpose to vets returning home with nothing to hold them together. It's why the initiation process is so long and thorough. I wanted to know the men in our ranks could handle the stress and be ready for the life we'd lead. Not everything in an MC is clean; even though I tried to get the despicable things that I knew would ruin a person far away, they'd sometimes slip through the cracks. A sweet butt would bring them to a new prospect thinking it was what we were about, or a visiting club would.

If we could've lived in a bubble and managed, I would've done it in a flash.

Part of the club business you don't know about is that we often work with law enforcement. Again, not something an MC is known for, but since many of us were from a military background, it was an easy segue. Half of our members are undercover agents, CIs, and a few US Marshals. Not everyone, but Tiny, Red, Bullet, and Brick are a few you're close with. It's the perfect cover for anyone needing inside intel, but without having to go so dark where they lose themselves in the process. Again, it's part of the weeding process the MCD program does. Everyone's results are sent to my contacts in the alphabet agencies, and they review them, flagging the ones they think might be good candidates. You and Maddox were primed to be in their ranks, but I messed up.

I'm not thrilled to have to say this to you, but I'm

not perfect. I know you'll find that hard to believe, but it's the truth.

I'll give you a minute to laugh.

I'd been given a mission to get close to Stanley Driscoll years ago. It hadn't been easy, but slowly, I'd been building a foundation with the scumbag. There were rumors he'd been dipping his toes in the sex trade business, more importantly, younger girls. Having a daughter myself, I couldn't let it stand, so I'd eagerly agreed to the task.

But I went too far. In my zealousness to catch him, I started to step over my moral line in pursuit of victory. My contact with the FBI wanted to pull me, but I begged them to give me one more chance. I was so close to being invited into his inner circle. Stanley gave me a test, though, and I failed. I'll spare you the details, but he didn't trust my motives and pulled away because of that. During this time, I made a massive faux pas of my own. I fell in love with Stanley's old lady.

I know it was wrong, and I regret it, but at the time, it felt right. But it had been a trap. She used me to get insider information of her own, taking a large portion of our club finances. Two strikes against me now, along with being on the verge of bankruptcy, I was desperate to change it all around.

Enter Agonizer and his deal. We combine our families—a union of our clubs. It would give us both more coverage, stabilize my finances, and guarantee the continuation of everything I'd built the Mavericks to be.

But when he said you had to marry his son and that he'd warm you up, I realized how far I'd fallen.

I'm so sorry, Peanut. I can never apologize enough for the mistakes I made. I got cocky and greedy, but none of that is your fault.

I decided I couldn't go through with the deal, and I told Stanley this. He was infuriated and threatened to take you anyway and put you in his program. I knew then he'd never tell me anything, that he was only using you as leverage.

That's why I'm writing this letter. I know I need to send you away. It's the only way I can save you, but it means I'll never see you again. You can't return to Mississippi ever again, Darcie. If you do, then I worry he'll swoop in and take you. I couldn't live with myself knowing it was my fault. At least this way, you'll have a chance at life, even if I never get to be part of it again.

I'm going to send Maddox with you. Not only is he a good man, but I know he cares about you and will keep you safe. When he was a teenager, he told me that he planned to woo you one day. I hope he still does. You both deserve happiness.

I've made many mistakes, but being your father was never one of them. Losing your mother changed me, and I miss her every day. I pray she wouldn't hate the screwups I've made, but I worry she wouldn't even know me. I hope this allows me to get back to the man that your mother loved. I want to be that version of myself again.

You are my light, Peanut, and I know wherever you go, whatever you do, it will be spectacular.

Trust no one else with your story. From this point forward, Darcie Callaway is a ghost. I've included some money, the name of my contact in the FBI if you ever find yourself in trouble, and the key to the safe deposit box that has all the information I've collected over the years on Driscoll. If anything ever happened to me, you have options. It's located at Music City Row Bank in Nashville, TN. Somewhere far away from here, where no one knows who the Mavericks or Hank the Tank is. It's a nice place. I think you'd like it there.

Love,

Your father

P.S. You're going to miss your road naming ceremony, so I think it's only fair to tell you what the club voted on. You were to be crowned Rosebud. Just thought you should know.

I blinked at the pages, so many secrets coming to light, and I didn't know how to process any of them. I laid the letter down, picking up a polaroid picture of my father, mother, and me. I was probably about five in the photo, squished between the two of them. God, how I missed my mother. She'd know what to do; she'd know how to help me.

I didn't know anything anymore. I didn't know if I even knew my father. If I'd known him at all.

Looking over at Maddox, I caught him watching me closely. "Did you know?"

He shook his head. "No. I knew your father had been up to something, but not what it was. We had a meeting to discuss my future next week, but I guess I won't be keeping that now." He stared off, thinking over the information. At some point, he'd pulled me into his lap, my shaking too much for him, and he held me to him as I read. I hadn't cared that he read over my shoulder. It was easier than having to repeat it.

"Where are we now?" I asked, needing to focus on something else.

"Outside of Memphis. Where do you want to go?"

"You know, you don't have to stay with me. You've fulfilled your agreement to get me out of there. You can go on and live your life." I said the words, but I didn't mean them. But something in me needed to feel the hurt, to crack open my heart and watch it bleed out. Maddox leaving me would do that. He was all that stood in my way to surviving at the moment. I didn't know if I should thank him or curse him for it.

My brain was messed up.

He tilted my chin, peering down into my eyes. "Princess, where you go, I go. You're mine. Don't you get it?"

I tensed, the words echoing around my skull. "No, I can't be. I'm too damaged." I shook my head, wanting them to leave me. I couldn't un-hear Agonizer saying it.

"Darcie, it's okay. I'll wait." Once again, he held his tongue, but this time, I was thankful. I think I knew what he wanted to say, and it would shatter me into a million pieces.

I wasn't lovable, and the sooner he realized that, the better.

But for now, I would cling to him, using his heart to remind myself mine still beat.

Diary #4

Dear Mom,

Did you know? I feel like you would. I'm not sure what to think. Why wasn't I told sooner? It makes things seem different, but also like nothing in my life is real.

I don't know where to go from here. Who am I? What do I do now? My life was mapped out in front of me—join the family business.

And now, I have no clue. What even is the family business? Spies? Snitches?

If you'd told me this, I probably wouldn't have believed you. Tiny doesn't scream under-cover material, but I guess that's the point. The least likely person is the best option.

I'm rambling tonight, but that's how my brain feels.

Maddox left me alone for the first time since it happened. It's been one week, but it feels like forever. At first, I was glad to have some space, but after thirty minutes, the darkness started to cover me. He's looking into a more permanent place for us. We settled in Memphis. I wish I could enjoy it more. I always wanted to come here, but the lights and sounds are all too much right now. It feels right, though. The blues of this place speak of things I feel in my bones.

What do you think I would be good at? I guess in a way, I get to reinvent myself, be a version of Darcie that wasn't raped. Yeah, I kind of like that.

Love,

Darcie

Five

DARCIE

y knee jiggled against the bed. It'd been two hours, and I was officially losing my mind. I picked up the phone and the card Chase had given me. It had a number on it and a symbol. How strange. Did he just go around and hand them out to girls? Was that how guys did it?

Hey, baby, here's my card. Give me a call.

I could just imagine the wink and finger point that went along with a line like that. No, it had to be for some other reason. Chase was a lot of things, but I didn't think he was one to have to hand his number out to girls. The boy was too hot for that.

Sighing, I typed it into the phone, hesitating. What would I say? Was it even a good idea? I knew Maddox would tell me not to, but there was the girl who'd been friends with him that felt I owed him at least a hello.

Yeah. Sure, Darcie.

ME: Hey

Wow, I really put myself out there with that one. Flopping back on the bed, I placed my hand over my head. If this was what girls went through when texting a boy, I was kind of glad I'd missed it. It was horrible.

The phone buzzed in my hand, and I practically jumped out of my skin. Sitting up, I opened it, my heart racing.

555-8394: Hey

Well, that didn't help. Ugh, I guess I had to be the one to use more words. Saving the number, a smile lit up my face. I just needed to remember to be someone else. Not *this* version of myself—fake it until I could make it, and all that.

ME: You've now been saved as Jackass.
ME: I just wanted to say thanks. I guess.
Jackass: Wow, I save you, and I get a title like Jackass. I'm offended, babe.

ME: I'm not your babe and I said thanks.

ME: You're a jackass for a whole lot of other reasons.

Jackass: Oh? Please list all the ways I've offended you, princess.

ME: Don't call me that. I'm not a princess. And that would take me all day.

Jackass: Fine, what can I call you then if I'm not allowed to call you babe or princess? I don't think it would be wise to save you under your name, considering my dad is on the warpath looking for you.

I sucked in a breath, biting my lip. Shit. He had a point, but the thought of Chase calling me a pet name felt too intimate, and that was too much for me at the moment.

ME: Call me Ghost.

Jackass: Feels a bit unfair, but fine.

Jackass: How are you? See, I'm not such a jackass.

ME: Fine. You're not always one, just 75% of the time. You weren't always that way, though. I remember you being sweet once.

Jackass: What? I'm always nice. I just keep it real.

ME: Sure. *eye roll emoji*

ME: I'm okay. Well, I'm not, but I'm trying to be.

ME: What happened after we left?

Jackass: When my dad woke up, he was furious and attacked your father. It took three men to pull them apart. Whatever deal they were brokering is down the drain, and I doubt our clubs will ever be friendly again. It's a shame, but since you're a ghost, I guess there wouldn't be anything for me there anyway.

Why was he saying these things?

ME: I can't really take you right now.

Jackass: I'm sorry, by the way. I hate what my father did to you. I hate to ask, but did you handle things?

ME: Yeah.

Jackass: That's one thing less to have to worry about. I couldn't imagine another miniature him in this world. Oh, gross. Nope. Not going there.

ME: You're weird.

Jackass: Better than being a jackass, I suppose.

ME: So, was my dad okay?

Jackass: He was pretty banged up, but

nothing that won't heal. Things weren't good, though, when we left. I think several of his men are mad he was going to bargain with you.

Jackass: I didn't know he was going to do that, you know? I don't need my father to get pussy.

ME: And there you go being a jackass.

Jackass: Ugh, fine. You might have a point. It's just so hard being good. It's much easier being an asshole who doesn't care about others. Take you, for example, if my father ever found out, I'd be a dead man. I'd much prefer to not have that hanging over my head.

ME: Sorry, your conscience means you might have to deal with your horrible father.

Jackass: You're right. It's just easier to think only of myself. Then no one can hurt me.

ME: That sounds like you've been hurt before. I find that hard to believe.

Jackass: There are a lot of things I imagine you don't know about me, ghost.

ME: You know I can hear you saying babe, even though you don't type it.

Jackass: I can't win with you.

ME: I bet that's a first.

Jackass: I liked it better when you'd just blush and lose all your words.

ME: Well, yeah, but we can't reverse time before your father raped me, so this is what you get.

Jackass: You're right. I'm sorry, it was a jackass thing to say.

ME: It really was.

I heard the key in the door, and I jumped. Quickly, I sent one last text before shoving the phone down my pants and attempting to act innocent. As soon as the door opened, my body moved on its own, and I flew across the room at him, wrapping myself around him.

"Oomph." His arms wrapped around me, bags crinkling in the process. "Miss me, Runt?"

"Mmhmm." I nodded into him. As much as I hated needing him, I did. Inhaling his scent one more time, I pulled away, straightening my shirt while I pretended to act normal. "So, did you find anything?" I played with the ends of my sleeves, avoiding looking at him.

"I think so. I want you to look at it and make sure you'll be comfortable there." He sat the things he'd gotten while he was out on the table, turning to look at me. I could feel his eyes on me. Unsure of my feelings, I debated telling him about my text conversation. I didn't think he'd want me to do it, but I also didn't feel right keeping it from him.

He didn't let me stay standing long as he picked me up and sat on the bed with my legs draped across him. Ever since Maddox had told me he had feelings for me, he'd been a completely different man. He constantly touched me, wrapping me up in his arms to be near him. I didn't mind it at all, needing his comfort more than I wanted to admit.

"What's up, Princess? You're being evasive, and since I know you better than anyone, something's on your mind. Do you not want to stay here in Memphis?"

"No, that's not it." I shook my head, my hair rubbing against his shirt at the effort. He tilted my chin up, and I almost drowned in his eyes. Sighing, I pulled the phone from my waistband. "I texted Chase."

I didn't know what I expected to see from him, anger perhaps, or even hurt, but all he gave me was a blank look. "And?" Maddox blinked, waiting for me to tell him more.

"I thought you'd be mad."

"Do I like the thought of you talking to him? No. But I'm not going to police who you can and can't talk to. That's not who I am. Now, if he was here and trying to hit on you again, you better believe I'd step in. But that being said, I can't forget that he helped us out in the end, and for that, I'll give him a pass until he does another asshole thing."

I giggled, opening the phone to show what I saved his name as. His face lit up and he moved, throwing me back on the bed. I bounced, laughing with him as he bent over me. The light overhead was blocked, and suddenly I was back in my bedroom with Agonizer over me.

"No, don't." I swung my arm, feeling my hand make contact with something as I tried to scramble out from under my attacker. This time I made it clear, and I scooted off the bed, landing on the floor. I kept going until I hit the wall. I sucked in a breath, holding my hands out in front of me. "Don't hurt me."

I took in a few lungfuls, sound returning to my ears, the pounding of my heart no longer the only thing I could hear. Blinking, I pushed the hair out of my face, looking down at my hands. Small divots from my nails were visible. Peering up, I found Maddox squatting in front of me, his hands stretched out in a peace gesture.

"It's okay, Darce. You're not there." He handed me a bottle of water, and I nodded, taking it. Sipping it, I felt the cold water run down my throat, the feeling soothing. Once I drank half of it, I pulled it away, sucking in a breath.

"I'm sorry. I didn't mean to hit you."

"It's fine." He smiled, holding in a laugh.

"What?" I asked, hitting him again.

"You hit like a baby deer, Darcie. It's not like you'd do much damage."

"Oh, really? That's what you think?" I dove for him, wrapping my arms around his neck. The momentum had him falling back onto the floor as I clung to him like a spider monkey. "I'll just squeeze you to death with my thigh muscles." I felt him laughing under me as I pressed. "Or better yet, tickle you!"

I let go of my arms and immediately began to tickle him. He placed his hands behind his head like he had all the time in the world. Huffing, I sat on his chest, debating what I could do. Tapping my finger against my lip, I pulled all my Maddox information to the front of my mind.

"So you're not ticklish on your ribs, but if memory serves me correct, you are on your feet!" I turned, scrambling down his legs to trap them in a vice grip so I could keep him from getting away, and I began to lightly stroke his foot.

"Don't, Darcie." His voice was stern, and I almost gave into the command, but the bratty side of me couldn't let him have this win. I needed to feel like I had control and wasn't a freak. Tracing my finger back and forth on his heel, I finally got a reaction when he tried to kick me away.

"Please, Princess," he begged.

"Say, Darcie's not a wimp."

"Darcie's not a wimp." He practically shouted it through his laughter, the ticklish feeling crawling up his throat. Letting go, I rolled off his legs, sitting cross-legged next to him. Slapping my hands together, I sat them on the top of my knees, looking at him triumphantly.

"Feel good about yourself?" he asked, sitting up and hiding his feet from view.

"I do, actually." Laughing, he stood and showed me the things he'd gotten from the store. We played Crazy eights around a junk food dinner that night, and I didn't feel so broken.

It was a start.

"What do you think we should do for jobs?" I asked, playing a card.

"Hmm, what do you want to do?"

I shrugged a shoulder. "No clue. I only know how to do the things I learned in MCD."

"Not true. You're great at a lot of things." He played a card, taking mine.

"Like what?" I asked, laying mine down next.

"You're an entertainer, you're friendly, and you make almost everyone feel at ease. You're great at math, doing lots of things at once, and making me happy."

"I make you happy?" I asked, looking at him from beneath my eyelashes. Something in me stopped, needing and dreading his words.

"You're my everything, Princess."

I sucked in a breath, trying to push his words away. I couldn't cope with them right then.

"So, basically, you're saying I should be a waitress?" I looked up, and for the first time ever, I saw his face fall. It was brief, but I saw the hurt flash across his eyes at my dismissal.

"Yeah," he cleared his throat. "That could work. I could do construction. We can look tomorrow and see what kind of jobs are out there. We have enough money to lay low for a bit, but I don't want to wait too long and then be broke."

"Sounds like a plan." I placed my card down, smiling. "I win." I smiled, but the mood felt different. "I guess we better head to bed so we can be ready in the morning."

"Yeah, sure."

Quietly, we got ready for bed, avoiding looking at one another. I felt like an ass, but I couldn't take his pretty words when I felt anything but inside.

We got under the covers, and I turned my back to him. "Goodnight, Maddox."

"Goodnight, Princess." A few moments passed before I heard him whisper, "I'll wait forever if I have to."

Closing my eyes, I pressed back the tears that wanted to fall. A week ago, I would've killed to hear a boy say that to me. Now I just felt empty. I both craved him and feared it.

What if forever wasn't enough? Would he still stay? Could I gamble with that?

Diary #5

Dear Mom,

Something isn't right in me.

Each time Maddox does something sweet and nice, I want to slap him for it. Why can't he see that I'm not deserving of those things? I'm damaged.

But then I think about them later, and I go all mushy inside. But when I'm faced with it, when he presents it to me or does something nice like buy me Starbursts, my favorite candy every time he's out, I just want to scream.

So, yeah, something isn't right with me. I'm broken. I'm wrong.

All my parts got mixed up, and I can't be put back together. I'm a mutant toy from *Toy Story*. Sid's gotten a hold of me, and instead of a body, I have spider legs. Instead of a head, I have a robotic arm. Instead of a heart, I have a hand.

How do I fix it when I'm unsure what needs to be fixed because it's all messed up?

Love,

Darcie

Six

DARCIE

The clink of dishes mixed with the chatter of customers had become the soundtrack to my days. Though, you couldn't forget the classic country tunes that played on the jukebox. It wasn't horrible as jobs went, but I often found myself wondering if this was it. Was this all my life had to offer?

I'd worked at the diner a month already, and I was itching for something new.

"Order up, sweetheart," the old fry cook hollered, dinging the bell. I laid the silverware I was rolling up to the side, walking over to the window.

"Thanks, Joe." I smiled sweetly, my face hurting from the gesture. Some days, I wondered how long I'd be able to hold up this fake sweetness before I cracked. By the end of the day, I'd walk home exhausted and want nothing more than to hide under my covers, pretending this wasn't my life.

But Maddox wouldn't let me.

He was both saving and drowning me. I didn't know which I wanted to win.

Sighing, I grabbed the food and walked it over to the table. "Here you go, sugars. Y'all be sure to let me know if you need anything else, okay?"

A hand started to roam up my backside under my uniform, and I froze for a second, the feeling making me want to hurl. The dark part of me snapped, reaching down to grab the hand that thought it was okay to touch me. Twisting the wrist, I pulled it free, raising it up over the table. The man winced, crying out.

"I'm not on the menu." I threw his hand back at him, turning to leave. I'd wanted to make him hurt worse, but the second I let go, reality crashed in, and I was on the verge of falling apart.

Making it to the bathroom, I locked the door behind me, and sank to the floor. Tears cascaded down my cheeks, and I scrubbed my hands on the apron I wore. No matter how hard I tried, I couldn't stop crying, the feeling of his hand left an imprint on my body.

Why did men think they had the right to touch me? Did I have a look about me that said they could?

A soft knock had me bolting up, wiping my face. "Darcie, sweetie, you okay?" Jodie asked.

"I'm good. Just a minute." I sniffled, wiping my face. I turned to the mirror, cursing my choice to wear makeup today. Splashing some water on my face, I sucked in a breath, holding it until I had to let it go. My hands shook as I tried to dry them.

Pulling my skirt up, I took my flesh between my fingers and pinched the area on my upper thigh. My legs were riddled with bruises. I knew I should stop, that it wasn't a healthy way to cope. But the pain was the only thing that helped me center myself, reminding me I was still here.

Once the bite of pain lessened, I let go, rubbing over it softly. Fixing myself, I held up my chin and headed outside, hoping I could make it through the rest of the day.

Another month passed, and things weren't getting easier. I woke up screaming, thrashing out as I tried to get away from my attacker. Maddox no longer slept in my bed when we moved into the tiny house we rented. He opted to sleep on the sofa, but he was always there to calm me when I woke in a panic.

Needless to say, we both looked like shit, neither of us getting any sleep.

He rocked me back and forth, smoothing my hair. "I'm sorry, Maddox." My body shook, and I whimpered as the tears fell. I hated feeling this way.

"It's okay, Princess."

"It's not, though. I'm tired of feeling this way. Make it stop, please."

I turned, cupping his face. Slowly, I leaned forward, touching my lips to his. He stayed frozen, not wanting to spook me. In the time since we'd been on the run, we hadn't kissed again. I'd thought about it, but each time I'd remember what came after a kiss, and I'd freeze up, not ready for it.

But maybe I'd been going about it all wrong? Darla had said something at work the other day that the best way to get over someone was to get under someone new. She was with a new guy every week, so maybe there was something to it.

I pulled back, staring into his eyes. "Will you," I swallowed, "will you give me a different memory? Please?"

Maddox froze, looking at me. "What?"

The response hadn't been what I expected, so I pulled back, feeling rejected. "Never mind. It's stupid." I turned, pulling the covers to crawl under them and die.

He touched my hand, stopping me. "Don't hide from me, Princess. Let's talk about this. It's a big deal, and I just want to make sure you're ready."

I turned back, some excitement filling me. "I just figured if I had another experience, maybe I wouldn't have as many nightmares. That the way to heal is to get back on the horse, so to speak."

He snorted. "Don't think I've ever been referred to as a horse before." He scrubbed the back of his head, running his palm over his hair. He blew out a breath. "Everything in me feels like this might be a horrible idea."

"Why?"

"I dunno. I don't want our first time, my first time, to be because of him," he whispered, dropping his head. I realized then what I was asking of him.

"Shit. I'm sorry. I just didn't think it would be your first. That's all."

"Well, yeah, it is." He peered up, looking at me, his cheeks red in embarrassment.

I crawled into his lap, wrapping my arms around his neck. I laid my head against his chest, listening to his heart. He laid back, pulling me with him, covering us both up.

"Forget I said anything."

"It's kind of hard to do that. What if we do it on our terms? Let's go on a date. I didn't want to push you with things, wanting to let you have some space before I threw my hat in the ring."

"Oh?" I asked, rubbing my hand over his chest. I smiled into him, a new feeling warming me, and I liked it.

"Yeah, Princess. I've been thinking about this moment for years. Let me romance you."

"I think I'd like that. To be romanced by Maddox King."

"Good. It's settled then. Now, sleep." He kissed the top of my head, and my heart started to race for a new reason.

Being romanced by Maddox King was romance on a whole other level. The morning after our talk, I woke up to a daisy and a note telling me I was beautiful and to have a good day. Each day after that, there was a new flower and a new note.

Sometimes they were funny one-liners; others were sweet messages. I kept them all in my journal, taping them to the pages until they filled it. I had twenty-one so far, and they'd become my favorite part of the day.

He'd also started walking me to work when he could or picking me up after. We'd walk hand in hand, talking about the most random things. It was a domesticated bliss I'd never seen for myself, but with Maddox, I liked it.

Swinging our hands, I smiled freely, the gesture feeling honest with him. "Do you think Joe and Jodie have sex on the back counter?" I laughed.

"I sure hope so. Often and lots. They deserve it."

"Oh, God, I won't be able to get that image out of my head now." I swatted his arm with my other hand, giggling.

"Hey, you brought it up." He narrowed his eyes at me, the sides crinkling as he tried not to laugh.

"Maddox! You're late."

I sighed, turning to see his boss leaning against his truck, undressing me with his eyes. I snuggled into Maddox's side, not liking the way his boss eyed me.

"Still got five minutes, Bill. I'll be there once I've kissed my girl goodbye." He waved, not bothered by the man. Maddox walked me the last two steps to the diner, stopping before the door. His boss was meeting him here this week before they headed out of town for a bigger job.

"I don't like him," I whispered, glad I couldn't see him anymore.

"It's a job." He shrugged, leaning down toward me. He was so tall he had to bend down or pull me up to kiss me.

Taking my face between his hands, he kissed me deeply, his tongue swirling with mine. My legs rubbed together, a slickness beginning to develop between them. His wanting to wait was both the best and worst thing.

It had given me time to heal some more, my body beginning to respond like it should, but the greedy hussy in me was ready to take it all the way. Almost a month of kissing, and I was about to combust.

"Be good, Princess. I'll be thinking of you all day." He kissed my lips once more before he spun on his feet, heading over to the idling truck. As soon as the door shut, the truck took off, almost hitting a car at his impatience. Shaking my head, I headed into the diner, not hating the day so much. It was a start.

Maddox was late, and I couldn't reach him by phone. Shoving my phone into my bag, I took off, deciding to check home. Maybe he wanted to surprise me with dinner or something and forgot to tell me he wouldn't be here.

I'd only been walking for a minute when Bill's

truck pulled up to the curb. I stopped, hoping it meant Maddox was here. Walking over, I peered into the cab, but I didn't see his smiling face. The window rolled down, and the driver leaned over. Bill.

"Hey, darling. Maddox sent me to pick you up. We got held up at the site, and he didn't want you to wait. I'm supposed to take you there."

"Why didn't he tell me?" I asked, crossing my arms. The hairs on my arms raised, not liking the situation.

"He dropped his phone earlier, and it busted all over the ground. Why he sent me, so you wouldn't worry. Come on, darling. Get in, and I'll take you to him. Nothing to be scared about."

"I think I'll just walk home and wait there. Thanks."

"Suit yourself, darling." His voice was stern as he gunned the engine, taking off.

Shaking off the weird encounter, I walked quicker, eager to be safe at home now. Something didn't feel right, but I didn't know if it was my paranoia or intuition.

Maddox hadn't made it home by dinner, and I was worried. It also meant I had to ask his boss where he was since he was the last one to know. Sucking it up, I made sure to wear jeans and a long sleeve shirt to cover myself before I headed out.

Using the bicycle we'd gotten at a garage sale, I made my way to the site. Maddox had taken me there last week on his motorcycle. It was a luxury suburb; the whole neighborhood would be half-million-dollar houses.

Some anxiety left me when I pulled up to the house and saw several cars there with lights on. Leaning the bike against a tree, I made my way up to the window, peeking in to see what was going on. It looked like a party was underway. Girls and guys were scattered throughout the room, red cups in their hands. I leaned forward, trying to find Maddox.

A body pressed me into the glass, and everything in me went into overdrive. All my training came rushing back, and I reached around, elbowing the person in the gut. Using the hand that had landed on me, I spun underneath them, stomping on their foot.

"What in the Sam Hill?" Bill cursed, looking at me like I'd lost my mind. He wheezed, rubbing the area I'd hit. "Dammit, Darcie. I was coming to ask you if you wanted to come inside. Maddox's there."

Sucking in air, I bent at the waist, trying to compose myself. "Sorry, you scared me."

He gave me an evil look, giving me a wide berth

as he made his way inside. I avoided looking at the others as I followed him, afraid they could see the crazy on me. He stepped into a room, holding the door open, motioning me in. I hesitated, not wanting to follow him in.

"He's inside."

He didn't step in, but stayed in the doorway. Making myself small, I stepped into the room slowly, apprehension filling me with each step. When the door shut behind me, the lock sounding, I knew I was in trouble. Instinct had me running for an exit, but a hand wrenched me back, pulling at my hair, dragging me to them. An arm wrapped around my throat, cutting off my oxygen.

Slowing my breaths, I tried not to panic as the body behind me held me close. Making my body a dead weight, I stopped pulling against him even though every instinct in me wanted to. Bill rubbed his groin into me, making me want to throw up.

No, this wasn't fair. Everything had been going so well. I was healing, and Maddox and I were creating something.

"Be a good little whore now, and we won't have a problem. You shake your booty all over town, so now it's time to pay the toll. Your boyfriend wasn't willing to take the discount, so instead of just me, you're going to lay there and take it for all my men. Understand?"

I stayed silent, not wanting to answer him as my plan of escape started to form in my mind. He kept talking, but I didn't give him anything back.

"The more you struggle, the more I'll enjoy it. Got it, darling?"

I waited for my moment. I wouldn't let another man take something from me. Not this time.

"No, I don't 'got it,' Bill."

Using every ounce of strength I had, I leaned forward and flipped him over me. His body went sprawling, and I used the moment of surprise to get away. It was all I had as I staggered to my feet to escape.

"You, bitch," he grunted, but I was already running toward the door.

I grasped the doorknob and was so close to freedom when something hit me over the head and it was lights out for me.

Waking with a splitting headache, it took me a minute to orient myself to where I was. I tried to move my arms but found them bound above me.

"Good, you're awake. I was getting bored."

The moment I heard his voice, everything came flying back to me. I tugged on the ropes, but it was to no avail. He'd secured them well.

The man climbed on the bed, straddling me. It was then I realized I was naked. Fear welled up in me, and I just wanted it to be over with. I was so tired of this.

Closing my eyes, I accepted my fate.

The door crashed against the wall and caused me to jump. I barely had time to open my eyes before I felt the body over me leave.

"Maddox." His name had never sounded so good.

His face was covered in rage, and I could spot some cuts and bruises on him. Had they tied him up to keep him from me? He kept punching the man, and I was suddenly worried we'd have a bigger problem on our hands if he killed him.

"We have to go, Maddox. We have to go now."

My voice pulled his attention, and he looked at me, sweat dripping from his brow. His eyes were wild, his breathing ragged. When I pulled at the bindings, he snapped and rushed toward me, taking a knife from his boot to cut them. Once I had one arm free, I felt better, not even caring I was naked in front of him right then. Maddox cut the last one, pulling me into his arms. I clung to him for a moment, needing to feel his solid presence.

"Come on, we need to get out of here."

He took off his shirt and pulled it over my head, helping to hide my nakedness. I didn't know where my clothes were, but I didn't particularly want to look at the floor either. When we walked around the bed, a moan snagged my attention, and my eyes fell to the man I'd wanted to avoid.

Before thinking about it, I reared my foot back and kicked him. It hurt since I didn't have a shoe on, but it felt worth it to hear him groan as my foot collided with his chin. Pulling my leg back one more time, I landed another kick to his groin, and he doubled over, moaning more.

"Help," Bill groaned, but I ignored him. "You won't get away with this," he wheezed.

"Watch me." Maddox pulled me into his arms, carrying me, which was much faster since my foot hurt. Still worth it.

"How'd you get here?" he asked, scanning the hallway and heading out in a different direction.

"Bicycle."

"Shit," he mumbled. "Okay, we'll have to leave it and jump his truck."

We stepped out into the night air, and I felt like I

could breathe again. My blood pounded in my ears, adrenaline racing through me.

"What are we going to do?" I asked.

Maddox glanced down, worry lining his brow. "I dunno. Leave, I suppose. I really don't know. I'm sorry, Darcie. I can't believe he tried that."

"Where were you? Why didn't you answer?" I asked, not knowing if I wanted the response.

His brow furrowed, and a harsh look crossed his face, but he shook his head, not wanting to tell me. I'd let it go for now, but I knew it was something I needed to know. I couldn't deal with secrets. Maddox opened the truck door, placed me down gently, and buckled me in. He shut the door and went around to the other side. He paused, walked back to grab my bike, and threw it in the cab.

I watched in amazement as he pulled the cover down and hot-wired the truck quicker than I could ask how we were going to get out of there.

"Okay, you've gotta show me that!"

Maddox glanced over, a smile spreading across his lips. "Sure thing, Princess."

He pulled out of the neighborhood, and we both sighed in relief, the energy-draining from me. My body began to shake as the adrenaline wore off, and I realized how cold I was.

"I really need to stop only getting your clothes

when I'm naked," I said, attempting to joke. It fell flat, Maddox's jaw tightening.

"You can have anything of mine, Darce."

I sighed. "So, where to now?" I asked, looking out the window.

"Let's worry about getting out of here first. Grab what you want to take with you, whatever will fit into a bag."

"Okay." My voice was small, but I knew it was the right choice. We couldn't stay here now. As much as I hated my job most days, I'd miss Joe and Jodie. They were friendly, and I liked them.

"I'm—"

His words were cut off by the red and blue flashing lights. We looked at one another, panicking.

"Just stay calm. I'll take care of it." I nodded, fear climbing up my throat.

The officer knocked on the window, shining a light on us. "Roll down the window, sir."

"Yes, officer." Maddox nodded, keeping his hands visible. "Can we help you, sir?"

He eyed us, shining the light on Maddox, probably checking his eyes. "License and registration."

"Well, here's the thing, officer. It's my boss' truck."

"I bet it is. License and registration." He shined

the light on me. "Real careful there, miss, reach in and grab the registration. No funny business, now."

"Of course, sir. We don't want any trouble."

We both pulled out the items he asked for and handed them over. He glanced at them, looking back up at Maddox.

"What happened to your face, son?"

"Construction accident."

"Hmph. I'll bet. I'm going to have to call this boss to confirm. Do you have a number?" Maddox froze, and I leaned over, rattling off the only number I knew, praying Chase would come through.

He wrote it down, tapping the truck. "Don't go anywhere."

Maddox glanced over at me. His jaw was tight, but he didn't ask whose number it was. It was probably for the best. The longer he took, the more I was freaking out. My hands shook, and I tried to remember what I could do to get out of this. When the officer came back, I was so hyped up I was sure I'd pass out.

"Here's a warning. Fix that taillight. Your boss said to call him."

Maddox nodded, taking back the items. We both sighed in relief as we went one way, and the cop turned in the other direction.

"I hate to ask what that just cost us," Maddox

said, gripping the steering wheel. I didn't know how to respond, so I didn't.

When we pulled into the house that had become our home the past few months, I knew nothing would ever be the same from here on out.

We were on the run. Again.

Diary #6

Dear Mom,

I don't know what to think anymore. Is life always this cruel? Are all men this despicable?

It makes me want to join a nunnery, if I'm honest. Dad would love that.

I'm trying to remember who I am and what I've learned. But not everything in the MCD program prepared me for this life.

At least I have Maddox. I wouldn't survive without him.

Love,

Darcie

Seven

MADDOX

Darcie snored softly next to me, and I ignored the outside world for a moment. For just a moment, I wanted to pretend this was real. That she and I had been able to make it in domesticated bliss, living a normal life.

I knew life would be hard away from the club, but I hadn't anticipated this. Without any backup or support, we were easy prey for the picking. I didn't like feeling this way, used to being the alpha dog in my world.

Sighing, I sat up, bracing my head in my hands. I had to do something. We couldn't keep running for the rest of our lives. It wasn't any way to live or helpful to Darcie. But what were my options? I couldn't leave her, even if it was better for her.

My life didn't make sense without my princess.

But I couldn't forget my purpose, my whole reasoning for joining the Mavericks in the first place. Avoiding reality and pretending I didn't have responsibilities wasn't doing either of us any favors.

And it wasn't just Darcie I was letting down, but the other piece of my heart.

Standing in resignation, I lumbered over to the dresser and pulled on my jeans, stepping into my boots. Snagging my wallet and phone, I stepped outside, closing the door silently. I walked over to the railing, peering out to the parking lot below. We were in some small town a few hours away. We'd need to leave soon, but I couldn't wake her just yet.

I unlocked my phone and stared at my contacts, my finger hovering over the number. I didn't want to make this call. Everything in my being was screaming at me not to. Resigned, I hit the button and placed it to my ear. It rang once before it was answered. Even in the early hours of the morning, he answered.

"I'm surprised to hear from you this soon."

"I know."

"What's happened?"

"There was an incident," I sighed, rubbing my forehead. "We're on the run." I hated to admit this to him because it meant I wasn't man enough to do it on my own.

"How bad?" he grunted, some papers moving around in the background.

"Possible assault and theft."

"What do you need?"

"I don't know. I'm grappling with what to do. She's struggling. I can't keep running from town to town. I don't think she'll survive it. But leaving her... it makes me want to rage out. I can't possibly do that."

"Hmm," the voice said, offering nothing else.

"What do you think I should do?" I instantly regretted the temporary show of weakness. Being away for so long had made me forget.

"Are you calling me for help or advice?" I heard what constituted as a chuckle from him. It was dark and low, rumbling through his entire body. But it wasn't out of delight for you, but for him. He was enjoying this.

"Both. I don't know where to go from here. I don't know if I can complete my mission. Things have been... compromised," I gritted out. It didn't matter that I wasn't talking about the same mission to him, but it was the truth. Everything had gone off the rails, and I wasn't sure how to get them back, or if I even wanted to anymore. Problem was, he wasn't going to forget his mission.

"Do you love her?" he asked, surprising me.

I rolled my eyes, not sure where he was going with this. I wouldn't sacrifice Darcie to him. "You know I do. That's not even up for debate."

"Then you need to do what's best for her, no matter what cost it is for you."

I stood there, silence engulfing me. It was surprisingly thoughtful coming from him. Destroyer wasn't known for his thoughtfulness. With a shaky breath, I continued, trying to figure out where he was going with this. "Even if that means she's alone?"

"Yes." I could hear the smile in his voice and knew this was what he wanted. Darcie made me useless to him. I hung my head. I'd known this would be the answer, but I'd hoped for something else. I shouldn't have been surprised, considering who I'd called. The Mavericks had made me believe in people again, but I wasn't dealing with the Mavericks any more.

"What do I do next, then?" I sighed, accepting my fate. I'd failed my mission, and it was time for a revamp.

"Get her settled, and then come home."

I sucked in a breath. Hearing him say the words made it more real. I hadn't been home in years, not since I'd passed the MCD program—it had been meant to be my ticket out. "I... But I haven't completed my mission," I stalled, hoping for a different response.

"It's time, Son. We'll figure something else out. You obviously weren't cut out for the job." I swallowed down the curse I wanted to make. Now wasn't the time. Perhaps this was for the best. I could take care of our problem, keep Darcie safe, and finish what I'd come here to do in the first place.

"What about the guy?" I asked, knowing if he didn't help here, we'd be screwed.

"Text me his name, and I'll take care of it."

"If you can do that, then why can't I stay with her?" I asked, not wanting to give in too quickly.

"You know the answer to that, Son."

Gritting my teeth, my hand tightened against the rail below me. Sometimes I really hated being the son of the leader of the notorious Chaos Gargoyles.

"Two days, Son. I expect you here in two days."

Opening the door, I was surprised to find Darcie sitting up in bed, the covers wrapped around her.

"Hey, Princess. I got breakfast." Sitting the bag down, I pulled out a bottle of chocolate milk and handed it to her. She smiled, but it wasn't her usual bright one. "What kind of donut do you want?" I opened the box, showing her what lay inside. I'd gotten all of her favorites, her eyes lighting up when she noticed. She selected a chocolate long john, taking a big bite before looking at me.

"Thanks, Maddox." She smiled at me around the bite, making my heart flutter.

"No problem. I have something to tell you, though," I sighed, rubbing my hands on my jeans.

She swallowed, taking a drink of her milk. I handed her a napkin, and she wiped her mouth, peering up at me. I hated how she looked like I was about to ruin her world.

"I have to return home."

"Okay. When do we leave?" I wanted to kiss her for saying that.

"No, Princess. Just me."

"But?" She frowned, dropping her head.

Sighing, I leaned forward, taking her hand. "My father is going to take care of Bill. I don't want your life to be running from one city to the next, always looking over your shoulder. You deserve better. The cost, though, is me returning."

"Why can't I go with you, then?"

"You know why, Princess." I rubbed my thumb over her hand. She shook her head.

"I don't accept that. I'd rather be on the run with you than without." Her eyes started to fill to the brim with tears, breaking my heart. Leaning forward more, I cupped her jaw in my hand, wiping the tears.

"I love hearing you say that. It means everything to me. But I can't forget why I came to the Mavericks, and you need to heal. Having to look over your shoulder every second isn't a way to do that. Coming home with me will only make you a bigger target, or even a new one."

"So, that's it then? You make this decision, and I have to go off and live on my own? What about what I want? What about what I can handle?" Her lip quivered, breaking my heart.

"Princess, this isn't easy for me! My father's club is a far cry from the Mavericks. You know how much I hate it there. You don't remember what he's like. Going there, I'll have to change, and I don't want you to see that."

"You're not trusting in us. You're not giving us the chance we need. If you can see past the darkness that coats me now after the vile things that have been done to me, then I can do the same. This isn't the answer, Maddox," she begged, her hands gripping mine.

"It has to be, for now, Darcie. It has to be. I have to make sure."

"If you do this, then I'll never forgive you."

I dropped my head, breathing deeply. When I

looked up, tears fell from my own eyes. "That breaks my heart, Princess, but it's a risk I'm willing to take to make sure you can become the best version of yourself. You don't need me hanging around, reminding you of what you've lost. I trust that we'll find our way back to each other."

"I hate you. Please, leave and take your pity donuts with you. I'll find my own way to wherever I want. I don't need you."

She turned, sobbing, and everything in me splintered. I didn't know if I could do this. Almost as if my father could feel me wavering, my pocket buzzed. Wiping my eyes, I stood and pulled out the phone.

Dad: Your problem has been taken care of.
Don't forget your window. Two days, or I will
send the squad after you. Don't run from me.
You don't want to risk that pretty girl of yours.

Hardening my heart, I pulled the last of the items I'd gotten for her out of the bag and placed them on the dresser. Walking over, I kissed her hair, holding her to me for a second.

"This isn't over, Princess. I refuse to say goodbye. I just have to make sure. I can't neglect my responsibilities and I think this is for the best. You'll see. Don't ever forget I love you."

She cried harder, and it took every ounce of strength I had to step away. Walking out the door, the click of it closing was like a bullet to the chest. Something in me had just been irrevocably damaged, and I prayed it could be repaired someday.

Climbing on my bike, I didn't look back. I couldn't. If I did, I'd surely turn around, committing us to a life of crime on the run, never safe. She deserved better, and maybe this way, we'd find it.

Pulling up to the battered compound a day later, dust mingled in the air, coating everything in a layer of grime. The Chaos Gargoyle logo was painted on the door, a sign to all to turn back unless you were prepared to enter the chaos.

The door swung open, the light cascading over the dark and dirty floor, hiding all that hid there beyond. It shut behind me, and a hand clamped down on me as I tried to blink, adjusting my eyes to the darkness.

"Welcome home, Son."

Diary #7

Dear Mom,

Men suck.

I wish I could like girls. It feels like it would be easier. A woman would never abandon me like this.

Part of me knows that he didn't, that he did what he thought was best, but it's small. So very small.

I know why he feels he needs to return home. But the bigger part of me doesn't care. Does that make me a selfish bitch? I needed him. He promised to be there for me, and now he's gone, and I have to figure out how to manage on my own.

I won't lie, the first few days, I stayed lying in that bed, staring at the wall. I guess

Maddox had anticipated this, paying for the room for a few days. But when the money ran out, they came knocking, and I realized how pathetic I was.

That and the woman looked at my state and said I could have an hour to shower and pack. It didn't take me that long since I only had two bags that hadn't been touched. I found an envelope and a package on the dresser in Maddox's handwriting, but I didn't trust myself to open it yet. So I shoved it down to the bottom of the bag with Dad's letter.

Seemed I had a thing for men disappointing me in letter form.

I'm on a bus now headed to the one place I'm hopeful my dreams will come true—Music City. Nashville had to be better than Memphis. Plus, it was at least close to the bank and information Dad had left me in case I ever needed it.

I don't want to admit that it felt kind of empowering to make it to the bus stop on my own, buying that ticket and deciding for myself. I'd been leaning on him too much, using him as a shield to protect me.

I know I'd needed it in the beginning, but I'd gotten used to his comfort, taking advantage of his natural tendency to take care of me. But I'd never tell him he'd been right. Nope.

I miss him, though. So much. His smell is everywhere, and I keep looking over my shoulder, thinking he just went to the restroom or to grab some food.

But he never returns.

That's the hardest part.

I want to be mad at him, but I can't. I love him. Funny how I realize that after he's gone.

I need to use this time, though, to become the strong girl I once was. I need to stand on my own two feet and figure out my shit. And hopefully, it will be time for him to return by then, once he's completed his mission.

I just know I can't keep waiting for life to happen to me. I have to start living it.

Nashville—here's to all my dreams coming true.

Love,

Darcie

Eight

DARCIE

Humming, I scrubbed the counter, dancing along to the song on the jukebox. My shift was about over, but then I had to head to my second job at the laundromat. No time to rest for the desperately poor in County Music's capital.

"You're good, Darcie. See you tomorrow." Jolene placed an envelope on the counter, and I sighed in relief. Tip payout days were my favorite. Sliding the thick envelope into my back pocket, I nodded, dropping the rag into the bucket, and headed to the back.

The Honkey Tonk bar was busier than the diner

had been, but it was fun. After getting a fake ID with the name Darcie Rosebud on it, I'd been able to find a job. This one was a cross between a bar and dance club with karaoke in between. They held several events that made it fun, constantly changing it up. I still wasn't close to anyone yet, but I was starting to feel like I could open that door.

"Night, Darcie," one of the girls said as I walked through the back room.

"Night." I waved, smiling softly.

"We're all headed to Layla's later if you want to join."

"Oh, I can't. I'm headed to my second job."

"Yuck! Girl, you work all the time."

"Yeah, well, gotta eat." I laughed awkwardly, not sure what to say. She eyed me a second before she walked over, stepping closer.

"What if I knew a way for you to make a lot of money?" She bit her lip, and I worried she was suggesting prostitution.

"Why does it sound like you're Pretty Woman-ing me?" I asked, raising my eyebrow.

She waved her hand, laughing. "Girl, that's so '90s. It's way easier than that now."

"Wait, so you are talking about prostitution? I thought it was a joke."

"I don't joke about this. And it's not prostitution. You don't have sex with the clients."

"Then what?" My brow furrowed, not understanding her meaning.

"Have you ever heard of a cam girl before?"

"No." I shook my head. I didn't think it was something I could do, but part of me was curious.

She smiled wide and handed me a business card. Did I miss that day in high school? What was with everyone having business cards now? It was black with "Candi" on it and a web address. I flipped it over, and the word "try me" was printed.

"If you're curious, go to that website and enter that password. You can get a free taste of what I'm talking about. I make bank now and only keep this job for the connections. I want to be a singer." She smiled, winking.

Cupping my hand around it, I nodded, sliding it into my pocket. "Um, thanks." She waved, heading out the other direction, leaving me standing, wondering what had just transpired between us.

I couldn't deny I was curious, though.

After six hours of standing on my feet at the laundromat, I was ready to crash into my bed. The whole time, the business card had burned a hole in my pocket. Each time a customer complained about a machine not working or that someone wasn't respecting the time limit on machines, it burned more.

Maybe it was worth a look? If it was online, it couldn't be that bad? Right?

Climbing up the rickety stairs of my studio apartment, I unlocked the door and stepped inside. My body relaxed, and I shuffled my feet over to the bed in the corner. My kitchen butted up to my living room, which included my bedroom, and ended with my tiny bathroom in the corner. It was the size of a shoebox, but it was mine, and I loved it for that.

But I wouldn't mind having more than one room for everything. You know, for all my shoes.

Grabbing some cold noodles out of the fridge, I sat down on my bed and kicked my shoes off, leaning back against the headboard. My body relaxed back into the pillows, and I let myself unwind fully. This was my safe place, my one area where I could be as strong or as weak as I felt. No one to judge me, no one to see. Just me.

It was comforting in a completely sad way.

My phone buzzed, and I pulled it out as I shoved a bite of noodles into my mouth.

Jackass: Hey brat, how was your day? You make it home?

ME: Yep. Eating some noodles.

Jackass: Cold, I bet. You're so gross.

ME: Not everyone can afford a microwave. I'm lucky to have a fridge and a hot plate.

Jackass: You know I can send you money.

ME: I know. Thank you, but no. I want to do this on my own. It feels important.

Jackass: And you say I'm stubborn

ME: No, I say you're a jackass. There's a difference.

Jackass: Haha

I smiled, happy to be talking to Chase. We'd weirdly enough become friends over the past few months. I'd finally called him when I'd gotten into Nashville and cried as I told him everything that had happened. He listened quietly and told me Maddox had made the right choice. I wanted to hate him, expecting him to say he was stupid, but he hadn't.

ME: I'm beat. I'll talk more tomorrow, loser.

Jackass: Always with such caring words there. Be safe, brat.

ME: Night, Chase.

Jackass: Night.

I smiled as I snuggled down into the pillows. They'd been the first extravagant purchase I made after my first paycheck. I could live in a tiny apartment where I basically showered and cooked my meals in the same space, but I needed good bedding. Placing the noodles on the nightstand, I pulled the covers over my head and fell asleep, the card still burning in my pocket.

The sun was setting when I managed to roll out of bed. Working through the night was an odd experience, but I started to crave it. I finally had a night off from both places, and a night in my PJs watching reruns sounded like a dream come true.

I wouldn't admit it was because I was too sad to have friends. Nope.

Taking a quick shower, I wrapped my hair in a towel and pulled on clean clothes. The one nice perk at the laundromat was unlimited washing for all of my things. It was one I took full advantage of. There was something luxurious about having clean towels whenever I wanted them.

Padding a couple of steps into the kitchen, I pulled out the frozen pizza and placed it in the toaster oven. While it cooked, I sat at my rickety table, opening the second-hand laptop I'd purchased last month.

The first thing I did was sign into the secure server and checked for any messages. When I saw the red light, my smile spread across my face.

It had taken me a while to remember I could communicate with people this way. It was just another reminder of what the trauma had stolen and the comfort bubble I'd been in with Maddox. I hadn't needed to think, so I hadn't.

I'd been hesitant about messaging him, but I needed to set something right. I didn't hate him, not by a long shot.

MadDog: Hey, @Rosebud. I saw a sunset today that made me think of you. I miss you, Princess.
Rosebud: @MadDog, was it ugly then?
MadDog: Ha, ha. How's your day? You just getting up?
Rosebud: Yeah. Long night.

We kept our lives vague, knowing it wouldn't be good for either of us if we overthought it. Instead, we rekindled our friendship, starting from scratch.

Maddox and I had never had a traditional relationship, so it made sense not to try.

MadDog: You doing okay?
Rosebud: I'm getting there. I miss you too.
MadDog: I know I'm not supposed to make promises….
Rosebud: Don't. It's too dangerous to hope.
MadDog: Okay
Rosebud: I talked to a girl at work.
MadDog: Oh? Gonna try to make a friend.
Rosebud: Yeah. I think so. You?
MadDog: I don't have friends here.
Rosebud: Yeah, I know. How's it going with your mission?
MadDog: I gotta go. Same time tomorrow, Princess?
Rosebud: Always.
MadDog signed out.

I didn't miss how he avoided answering. Clicking over to the other chat I had, I sighed when there wasn't a new message.

Rosebud: Hey, Dad. I love and miss you. How are you?

I signed out and checked my accounts with nothing else to do on the site.

Checking Balance: $300
Savings Balance: $100

Along with the money from last night, I had roughly $500 to my name. It wasn't enough. Rent was due next week, and I'd barely be able to cover it. Exhaustion covered me, sitting heavy on my shoulders. I guess I could ask for more shifts or get another job.

Looking over my space, my eyes snagged on my jeans, and I hopped up, remembering the card. Pulling it out, I held it in my hand, debating if I was that desperate. Glancing around my place, the tiny amount of food I had, and the constant hunger I was in—yeah, I was that desperate.

Sitting back at the table, I typed in the web address, surprised when a black website came up. It had a picture of a seductive girl on it and a box to the side asking for credentials. Using the drop-down menu, I was surprised there were so many names. Landing on Candi, I hit select and then typed in the word on the back.

The screen flickered, revealing a page of videos. Most were locked and showed they cost anywhere from $5 to $25 to watch. *Shit.* A blinking light at the top pulled my attention, and I saw it said a live video was in progress. Clicking on it, a screen popped up.

Would you like to use your free five-minute access now?

Clicking yes, I held my breath, not sure what to expect.

When she came onto the screen, the angle was of her from the bust-up. She wasn't naked but had on a skimpy robe that was see-through, practically giving anyone a visual of her breast if they looked close enough. It was erotic without nudity, I supposed. I realized she was talking about what she should make for dinner. When I noticed the chat screen and all the messages popping up.

So, it was like an interactive thing? I didn't know if I liked that. Felt like a lot of pressure. The more I watched, though, I realized she was just talking about everyday things and getting paid to do it. She'd ask opinions and give people the option to pick for her if they tipped. I watched as dollar bill signs and hearts flew up as she zoomed out, getting up to walk into another room. I immediately gasped when I saw her state-of-the-art kitchen.

"Okay, now I'm jealous."

My own pizza dinged, and I pulled it out, realizing how pitiful it looked compared to what she was making on-screen. Candi pulled down bowls and ingredients, all while practically naked, talking to people. I guess it wasn't too bad. A timer flashed up, and I found I was actually kind of disappointed. A message flashed, and I found myself tempted to say yes.

Would you like to continue for $5 for ten minutes?

Hitting no, I clicked back out to the main page and decided I wanted to see the whole picture before deciding if this was something I wanted to do. I found folders and clicked on a few.

Cleaning

Cooking

Bathing

Talking

Private chats

NSFW

I was half tempted to click on the NSFW ones, but I didn't want to see that of my coworker. Clicking on the cleaning one, I coughed up $5 and selected a video with the most views. Candi stood in a bra, thong, and high heels. She waved at the camera and then set it down on a stand. She came on explaining how dirty her apartment was, and then she vacuumed. Legit vacuumed. And got paid for it. Shit.

Could I do this, though?

Deciding I needed to see the NSFW ones, I clicked

back to the main screen and selected a different name —a male one. Patrick's screen loaded, and my hand hovered over the folder, shaking slightly.

"Just click it, Darce. He's not going to bite. He can't touch you."

I clicked on it, taking a deep breath, and hundreds of videos loaded, ranging from $5 to $100. *Damn, Patrick, get it.* Selecting a cheap one, I pushed back from the table, needing some space from the screen and me. It was irrational, but it felt the further I was from the screen, the more control I had.

He came on, his face not in view, just him sitting on a bed with tight white boxers, his erection visible. I gulped. Okay, so far, not so bad.

"Hey, you."

I jumped, his deep voice surprising me. He chuckled, and it felt like he was right there with me. Wow. I looked over my shoulder to make sure, even though I knew he wasn't. I still checked.

"I'm so glad you could join me today. Are you ready to get a little naughty, lover?"

He rubbed his hand over his length, and I watched in amazement as it grew.

"Yeah, that feels good. Fuck, I'm imagining you being here, rubbing me. Do you want to see it? Yeah, you do."

I found myself nodding, despite being scared.

Slowly, he rolled his briefs down, his thick erection jutting up from his underwear. He stroked it once, squeezing, and I sucked in a breath. Shit. It was kind of hot watching him.

"That's it. It feels so good. Do you like watching me? Touch yourself for me. I want you to feel good while you watch me."

I thought about it, my breathing quickening, but I was too shy, afraid he could see me somehow. Instead, I watched, learning from him as he pleasured himself. His breathing quickened, and right before he was getting close, another screen popped up, telling me I needed to purchase more time to see the finish.

My breathing was shaking, and my insides rattled, and somehow it took all my willpower to hit no.

I understood now. It was erotic watching someone, getting a peek into their private life. It felt like I was right there with him. Yet, I wasn't. It was safe and controlled. And with the pay scheme how it was, it would be easy to make more money in one night than I did all week. If I was poor and was tempted to give up money for a few more glimpses, imagine people who were well fed and horny.

Tapping my fingers on the table, my pizza sat discarded, cold now. Pulling out my phone, I texted my boss for Cathy's number. I had to stop myself and not use Candi.

> **ME**: Hey! I wanted to switch with Cathy.
> Could I have her number?
> **Boss**: Sure. One sec.
> **Boss**: 555-5883
> **ME**: Thanks
> **Boss**: Any chance you want to come in
> tonight?

I debated, always willing to pick up any shift in the past. But this was my first night off in ages, and I didn't have it in me to go. Plus, if I decided to do this, I wouldn't need it. Taking a gamble, I said no for the first time in forever.

> **ME**: Sorry, I can't. I'll see you tomorrow.

Texting Candi, I sucked in a breath as excitement coursed through me. I was nervous as fuck, but maybe this could be the next step for me to gain control. It would be nice not to have to eat ramen or pizza for every meal.

> **ME**: Can you tell me more? I'm interested.
> **Candi**: Yay! Sure thing, girl. Want to come

over?

ME: Um, yeah, okay.

Candi: Sweet. See you in a few!

She sent her address, and I found myself jumping up to throw clothes on. This was happening; this was really happening.

That night, I listened to Candi tell me the details of being a cam girl and how it worked while we ate the dinner she'd just made with strangers, practically topless.

"So, you get to control what you do?"

"Yep. You can do as little or as much as you want. Show as much or as little as you want. Just no falling in love with the clients or sleeping with them; that's the one no-no. Kind of like stripping. You can't do your best if you're in love and a jealous boyfriend/girlfriend is a mood killer."

She dipped her fork into the bowl, twirling noodles around it, taking a bite. Candi was the type of carefree I wanted to be. She owned her sexuality and wasn't ashamed of it. I wanted to be like her.

"So, what do you think, girlie?" she asked, sitting up and looking at me.

"I think I want to try. I might not be any good at it, but it beats cleaning lint out of dryers at 3 am."

"Yay!" She jumped up, moving to hug me. "This is going to be great."

I smiled, hoping she was right.

She helped me pick out a look, letting me borrow some of her clothes. Together we created my account and set me up as Rose. It was time for Rosebud to bloom.

Diary #8

Dear Mom,

I'm trying something. I'm not sure if you'd approve or not. We didn't really get to have these kinds of talks before you died. I like to imagine you'd be open and progressive, telling me to explore and figure out what I want.

While that's part of why I'm doing this, I think it's also the way forward for me. Not only because I'll actually be able to keep living, but I think I'll be able to get something back that was taken from me. That's my hope anyway.

My only hesitation is Maddox. I don't know what to say to him or how to tell him this. We're not anything to each other, but that also feels like a lie. We were just getting started when everything stopped, and now I don't know when I'll see him again.

Do I wait?

Is he?

Should we talk about that? Probably.

Will we? No. It's not part of the agreement.

So why do I feel like I'm lying to him? I don't know how he'd take it.

I think if he was okay with it, it would break my heart. At the same time, if he's all jealous and demanding, it would break my spirit. I'm doing this for myself, so maybe I just need to keep it to myself. For now, that's what I have to do anyway.

Tonight is my first live. Let's hope I don't vomit, pass out, or freak out.

Love and miss you, Mom,

Darcie

Nine

DARCIE

Twisting in the mirror, I checked out my outfit one last time. It was a corset top with thigh highs. I was covered more than my previous bikini, but this felt more provocative. I pulled my hair up, getting it out of the way, and applied some lipstick. I kissed the air in the mirror, pursing my lips, trying to channel my alter ego.

"It's now or never, Rose."

I checked my computer, making sure it was ready to record. I'd need to get some better equipment, but for now, it was all I had. So far, I'd uploaded ten videos of myself doing random things around the house or talking about nonsense. They'd gotten decent hits, and I'd made a hundred dollars so far. It had taken me a week to get them done, and the rent was due, so I was sucking it up and doing a live video.

Candi had told me it was how you built your fan base, by interacting with people. I hoped it was true because I needed this to take off more if I was going to survive. The money I made was nice, but it wouldn't keep me from being on the streets.

Positioning the laptop so I didn't show my face, I got on the bed and tried to look sexy. Taking a deep breath, I leaned forward and hit the live button. There was a delay, so I scooted back and made sure I was clear of the camera for the millionth time. I was lying on my stomach, my feet in the air behind me. With the angle, it was a great cleavage shot.

At first, I was just sitting, staring when no one joined, unsure if I should talk or just wait. After a few minutes, it began to show me people were viewing. Swallowing, I waved and tried not to fidget.

"Hi, y'all. I'm Rose." I cleared my throat. "Thanks for tuning in. This is my first live, and I'll be honest, I'm kind of nervous."

Some messages popped up, and I looked down to read them.

"Hi, @livingfast and @ogbobbuilder. Thanks for joining me. Do you guys have any questions?"

They typed some more, and I found it easier with direct things to concentrate on.

"What's my favorite color? Hmm, good question. I think I like rose gold." I smiled, even though they couldn't see it. Candi had mentioned people could hear it in your voice, and I wanted to come across as friendly. A few more questions began to filter through, and I found it easier to talk to the screen like we were having a conversation.

Instinctively, I found myself playing with my necklace, drawing their attention to my boobs more. When tips and likes were given, I realized that the more I gave them, then the more they'd give me. An idea popped into my head, and I wanted to see if it would work.

"So, guys, my time's almost up tonight, but maybe you could help me since I'm still new. I'm going to put a poll up, and whichever option gets the most tips, then that's what I'll do. The options are should I play the guitar, make dinner, or paint my toenails? You have one minute."

I typed it into the chat and sat back, watching as people started placing their votes. I smiled, adrenaline coursing through me. At the end of the timer, I was surprised that the winning option was to play the guitar.

"Okay, thank you, @trentbulldog, for that last generous tip that put guitar over the top." I blew a kiss to the camera. "Well, that's all tonight, but I'll be back later and play the guitar for y'all. Ciao!"

I kissed the air, waving. It had been risky to show part of my face, but it had felt worth the risk when tips had come in more for it. Signing off, I looked down at the total, and my eyes bugged out.

"Holy shit. Candi is a freaking genius!"

Thirty minutes live, answering questions with twenty people watching, and I'd made over $500 in tips. I blinked, not sure it was real. Rolling over, I kicked my feet in the air, giggling as I screamed out, relief settling in my body.

I'd done it. I'd found a way to survive all on my own.

Strength and accomplishment raced through me, filling me with pride. A message pinged, and I rolled back over to check it. My inbox flashed, and I clicked on it.

@shycowboy sent you a message

I clicked on the message, squinting in case it was a dick pic. Candi had warned me about those. Instead, it was a message. Blowing out a breath, I leaned closer to read it.

Dear Rose,

I debated reaching out to you but thought I'd say hi.
I think you're beautiful and I hope we can get to know

one another. You seem like a sweet girl, someone I wish I could meet in real life. Hope that doesn't sound creepy.

Shy Cowboy

For some reason, it made me blush, and I tapped my finger, debating on responding. I remembered Candi's two rules: Don't fall in love and never meet them.

Surely it wouldn't be a bad thing to just message, right?

If anyone asked, I'd blame it on hoping I could make a client out of him. In reality, I was lonely, and it was someone to talk to.

Dear Shy Cowboy,

You flatter me. I'm sure there's a girl better than me around the corner. She'll surprise you one day. Thank you for your message.

Rose

Wow, Darcie, that was lame. Sighing, I signed off, exhaustion filling me. This had been a good start, and I felt more confident this could work. Baby steps, but it was at least in a new direction, far away from the girl I'd been.

It had been a month since my first live, and things had progressed well. I did them a couple times a week now unless I was too tired from work. I'd also started having some one-on-one sessions with clients. Most importantly, I'd earned enough to move to a new place.

It wasn't the biggest, but it had a great location, and everything had its own room. No more sharing space with my kitchen or bathroom. There was even a tiny laundry unit that I was excited about. No more trips to the laundromat, hauling my clothes. It was going to be the height of luxury for me.

Tonight was my last night doing a cam session in this place, and I felt a little tearful about it. Though, not enough to stay. Setting up my new camera, I adjusted the angle and laid back on the bed. It had a remote control with it so I could position it easier.

I'd kept talking with Shy Cowboy, and we'd been more flirty the past few times. He'd asked me last night if I'd be willing to do a private session with him. I wanted to say no, but I knew I needed to push myself. So I'd agreed.

Nerves were starting to get the better of me, though, but I reminded myself that it was Shy Cowboy. It wasn't a real person I knew, but someone I'd gotten to know. It wasn't a stranger, but it wasn't someone I had to face afterward either.

Taking a breath, I hit play on the music. I knew I needed to get in the mood a little before our videos connected. I hoped the music would help drown out the thoughts. Soft tunes came on, helping to ease my anxiety.

Closing my eyes, I drifted my hand over my breast, feeling okay. I was worried the moment I had to do more, though, I'd freeze up. So I trailed my hands down over my body, getting more comfortable. Breathing heavily, I felt ready and looked over at the time. The screen showed he was already in the private room, so with a shaky hand, I hit the button.

"Rose?" he said, his voice filling my ears. It was soft, smooth, and deep.

"Hi, Shy Cowboy."

"Hi." He chuckled, the sound bringing goosebumps to my skin. "You can just call me Cowboy if that's easier."

"Sure, I can do that. How are you?" I wasn't sure how this worked, but it felt odd to just jump into the sexual stuff.

"I'm good." I watched as he came more into the camera, keeping his face hidden. I'd been expecting a scrawny guy, or maybe an older man, figuring that was who was on these sites. I hadn't been expecting a younger guy with a body like his.

"Shit, you're hot," I blurted, immediately slapping my mouth. "I'm sorry. I didn't mean to say that."

He laughed, the sound doing funny things to my insides. "Shit. If you could see my face right now, it's so red." His country accent was thick, and I liked the way it sounded. When we stopped laughing, he cleared his throat. "So, I have a confession."

"Yes?" I asked, placing my head on my hand. I was lying in bed in a red bra and panties. It was simple, but I thought it looked good on me.

"I've never really done this before. I mean, I've done stuff with girls, but I mean here, online. However, if I'm being honest, my experience is limited with girls. My name is pretty accurate. I'm shy in real life, and I usually talk myself into twisted nonsense with girls as pretty as you."

"Well, believe it or not, I'm not that experienced either." I bit my lip, hoping he wouldn't hold that against me.

"Really? I'd never be able to tell. You always seem so confident."

"It's just me stepping into that persona. Or, I guess I am confident in general, or I was at one time." My voice trailed off, going quiet. "Anyway, so we both are new to this. You're my first private session."

"Wow, really? I'm kind of honored."

"Good." I smiled. "So, what do you want to do? Do we just like talk, or, you know?" I asked, laughing a little.

"It's kind of freeing to know you don't have expectations. Would it be okay if we just talked for a little bit?"

"Absolutely." I wanted to say he was paying for it, so we could do whatever, but I didn't want to cheapen it. "So, what made you try Cam Girls?"

"It seemed like an anonymous way to become more confident."

"That makes sense. So, what do you do?"

"Well, would you believe it if I told you I was a cowboy?" He laughed, and his southern drawl became my favorite sound.

"The name makes more sense then." We talked for ten more minutes, things becoming more relaxed. "So, Cowboy, if this was a real date, what would you do right now?" I asked.

He cleared his throat, taking a breath. "Assuming this is the version of myself that doesn't screw things up, then I'd kiss you."

"Oh? That's a good place to start. How would your lips feel on me?"

"Hm, hard, but soft. I'd want to taste you, but wouldn't feel like I had enough time."

I sucked in a breath, his description entrancing

me. "That sounds nice. What would you do next after this kiss?"

"I'd want to touch you all over."

"Like this?" I asked, skating my hands over my breasts, trailing it down my stomach.

He swallowed. "Yeah. You're so beautiful, Rose."

"Thank you, Cowboy. You know, you're not so bad at this. Where would you want me to touch you?"

"Oh, um, I don't know. I usually focus on the girl because I'm so afraid she's going to run away."

I laughed a little. "Oh, Cowboy. This is a fantasy, so let's both get some. Show me where you'd want me to touch you and how."

"Okay." He gulped and moved his hands down his stomach. I watched as he rubbed his hand over his boxers. It was hard to see since he was sitting mainly in the dark, but I could make out his shape.

"How far do you want this to go?" I asked, slipping a strap down.

"Um," he paused, focused on my fingers. "What are you comfortable with, Rose?"

It was the first time a man had ever asked me that I realized. I stopped, thinking about it. I looked on the timer and saw he had twenty minutes left.

"What if we show whatever we both feel comfortable with since it's our first time?"

"Yeah, I'm good with that," he said, shaking his head. I still couldn't see more than his chin, but every now and then, I'd catch his movement.

I sucked in a breath, dropped my other strap, and pulled my bra off. Slowly, I moved it to the side and brought my hand back to my breasts. I was too nervous to look at the screen, though. If I just focused on myself, then it didn't feel so scary. To be honest, it didn't feel as terrifying with Cowboy.

Pinching my nipples, I finally decided to brave it and looked up. His hand was inside his boxers, stroking himself. I thought I'd be indifferent to someone else pleasing themselves, figuring I'd have to go to a place in my mind to get off. But as I watched him fist his cock, stroking it as he looked at me, it did something for me.

Slipping my hand down, I dipped my fingers into my panties, touching my clit. I moaned at the touch, forgetting where I was. I watched him as he pulled himself free, and I sucked in a breath at his length. My fingers dipped into my core, my juices coating me as I found myself climbing toward a release I didn't think was possible.

"Oh, shit," I said. "That's hot."

"Hearing you say that makes me want to blow. You're one to talk, Rose. I think you're the most beautiful girl I've ever seen. Watching you is the best experience of my life."

"You're a sweet talker, Cowboy. I'm close. Cum with me."

I sped up, plunging deep as I rode my own fingers. I was surprised at myself for being able to do this, but it felt safe. I was in control here, and I did trust Cowboy to some degree. He let me lead the session, choosing to do what I was comfortable with, and didn't make me feel like I owed him anything. Even if he was paying me. It did wonders for my healing.

Crying out, I tightened around my fingers as I came. I was barely able to keep my eyes open as I watched him come, his release squirting out in jets onto his stomach. Those delicious abs that I wanted to lick now.

The thought surprised me, and I found myself pulling back, needing some space.

"Wow, that was um, yeah," I mumbled, feeling embarrassed now.

"No kidding. I don't think I've ever cum so hard. It makes me wish this was real, you know. But even still, it was the best experience of my life, Rose."

His voice was so kind, so awestruck, that the humiliation disappeared.

"You're welcome, Cowboy. Have a good night."

"Bye, Rose."

"Bye, Cowboy."

I turned off the camera, shut the laptop, and I laid back in the bed, replaying everything. I just had my first consensual sexual experience, and it hadn't sucked. It only took about ten months, but I felt like I was finally on my way toward healing. And a shy guy named Cowboy had helped me get there.

Diary #9

Dear Mom,

I can't believe it's been a year since every-thing happened. I miss Dad. I wish I could talk to him. I miss his hugs and his voice. I want to know how things are, but it makes me worried that it would be worse to know.

I miss Maddox too. Even if nothing ever came of us, I miss his friendship. He was that shadow, that looming presence who was always there, watching over me. Our chats aren't the same.

I miss motorcycles. The noise, the smell, the way they feel between your legs. The power I had riding on one. I miss it all.

But when I'm not missing things, I'm able to see the things I've gained as well.

I'm not the same girl I was a year ago, and not just because of the things that happened that night. I'm stronger now. I've been able to make it on my own, and I'm finding out things about myself I never knew.

For instance, I love to dance and sing. I'm also pretty good at teaching others. When I get out of my head, I can be entertaining. I'm finding new paths and what that might mean for me. It's exciting.

Another thing, I'm a horrible cook. The absolute worst. If it doesn't go in the microwave or oven, I will ruin it. Even those are iffy on if I'll burn them, but I have a better chance.

I'm learning how to make friends with people and not be such a recluse. I'm kind of funny when I'm comfortable.

Being active is something else that's important to me. I was always busy at the club but thought it was just a product of my upbringing. But I thrive off it. If I'm idle, I feel lazy and slip into the negative space my mind can become. It's not good for anyone when that happens.

Now that I have money to live, I've taken some classes. I started with self-defense, but it wasn't anything I didn't know from MCD. So after one class, the instructor recommended a more advanced course. So, now I'm taking Krav Maga, and I love it. It challenges me, uses my body, and makes me capable of protecting myself. It's been a huge help in my healing, along with the things I do on screen.

I started a dance class this past month, and it's been a blast. I wanted something fun for myself, and it's helped me learn how to move my body as well, helping with my confidence.

This brings me to the most significant area of my life. Being Rose is addicting. I can be whatever version of myself I want when I'm on screen. At first, I didn't get that, and I was shy and timid. But after my time with Cowboy, I began to see I didn't have to be Darcie with all of her hangups, but I could borrow some of my confidence and embrace the best parts of Rose.

It's also nice having people tell me I'm beautiful and spend money to just talk to me. I know it's not something I can do forever, but it's been what I need right now. A safe way to explore and be sexual without having to be sexual. It makes sense in my head.

I'm happy with where my life is headed,

but I miss you, Dad, and Maddox. Even Tiny and Red. I know I can't go back, but it doesn't make it any easier. Sometimes I get so tired of missing people.

I'm going to a new place tonight with some friends. It should be fun. It will be good to get away from the computer. Because I don't want to admit that I've become attached to a few clients, and I know that's not good. It's a fantasy, and I need some reality.

Time to boot, scoot, and boogie.

Love you, Mom

Darcie

Country music blasted around me, and I swayed to the music. I had a pair of tall cowboy boots on, cut-off denim shorts, a Dolly Parton tee, and a long cardigan. The leopard print cowboy hat was the final touch. I felt comfortable and sexy, my favorite combination.

"Darcie, come dance!" Candi called from the floor. Rolling my eyes, I sat my glass down and headed toward her. Cutting between people, I squeezed into their line, finding some space. We were at a line dancing bar. It was fun, and I'd been dancing and laughing with my new friends all night.

"This is so much fun. We should do this at the bar!" Candi said, raising her eyebrows seductively.

"Good luck with that," I teased.

Ever since I'd gone over to her place, Candi and I

had become close. She'd been pulling me along with her and her friends ever since. They were easy to like, and I always enjoyed my time with them. It felt nice to be part of a girl group, something I'd never had before. I didn't know what the teen movies were on about; they were all nice.

The song ended, and we clapped, the instructors announcing they were taking a break. Music came on over the speakers, and we headed off the floor to grab some drinks. Leaning against the counter, I looked around at the crowd. It was mostly people in their twenties with a few older couples who were line dancing die-hards.

Drinks were placed in front of us, and the bartender nodded down to the end where two guys sat, staring at Candi and me. "Courtesy of those gentlemen."

We raised the drinks, thanking them. "What do you think?" she asked, taking a sip. "You want the blonde or the ginger?"

"Um." I bit my lip, anxiety crawling up my throat. "Whoever." I shrugged but didn't put any effort into it. This was the part I always hated. Guys were constantly hitting on her, and by association, me. They'd buy us drinks, chatting us up. Candi loved it and would go home with a different guy each time. I couldn't seem to get over that threshold yet. I'd had plenty of sessions online now, but when it came to in person, I was still blocked.

"I'll take the ginger then. He has something sexy about him," she said, biting her lip. "Come on." She pulled me over there, and I went, dread filling me.

"Hello, boys. Thanks for the drinks." She flirted like the best of them.

"No problem. Two drinks for two of the prettiest girls here," the blonde guy said. He wasn't ugly, but he wasn't doing anything for me either. I smiled kindly, though, not wanting to be rude.

"Want to dance?" Candi asked, pulling the redhead's arm toward the dance floor before he could answer. The other guy looked at me, and I shrugged, tossing back the drink and headed to the floor.

His hands landed on my hips as we settled on the dance floor. He wasn't a horrible dancer, and our bodies found a good rhythm together. I guess there were worse ways to spend the time. When the song ended, I turned to ask Candi a question and found her making out with the guy.

"Well, okay then." The guy I'd been dancing with chuckled, pulling me off the floor. I went, not sure what else to do. He led me to a quieter area and grabbed some water from a passing waiter.

"So, what's your name, twinkle toes?"

"Darcie. Yours?"

"Rick."

"Nice to meet you, Rick."

"You don't like me, do you?" he asked, smiling.

"No, it's not that." Panic rose in me, and I tried to fix the situation.

"Darcie. It's okay. I kind of like you more because of that, which is bad for me, but you have nothing to worry about. Plus, the tall guy giving me death stares while we danced was a message to keep my paws to myself."

"Tall guy?" I asked, looking around but couldn't see anyone. Sometimes it sucked being short.

Rick laughed. "Do you need a ride home or anything? I think our friends are going to hook up, so I didn't want you to wait on them."

"Oh. That's really kind of you. I'm good. Thanks, though. Uh, it was nice meeting you, Rick." I waved awkwardly and then started to walk off.

"You too, Darcie." I smiled, respecting him more, and waved bye.

I stepped outside, the night air not much cooler than inside. Summer in the south was like a constant state of stickiness. Humidity—the devil's favorite punishment.

It wasn't too late, but I was tired, so I texted the girls that I was heading home so they wouldn't worry. The streets were still filled, the city full of people looking for someone to spend the night with. My feet were hurting by the time I stomped up to my stairs. I was only on the second floor, thankfully, and the walk hadn't been too far. The bar we'd been at was only about ten minutes from me.

I pulled out my keys and inserted it into the lock when someone stepped out of the shadows. "Darcie."

Screaming, I jumped back, dropping everything. I clutched my chest, trying to get my heart to calm. When I realized who it was, I wanted to dive into his arms, but nine months of not seeing someone made me hesitate.

"Maddox. What are you doing here?"

He bent down, grabbed my keys, and put everything into my purse. I noticed the stamp on his hand, and the comment Rick made suddenly made sense.

"You were at Wild Horse Saloon, weren't you?"

He froze for a moment, but then finished stuffing everything in and stood up, handing it to me. "We need to talk."

"Fine. I've been trying to for months." I finished unlocking the door and stepped inside, motioning for him to enter. He brushed past, his arm skating across mine, and my whole body came to life. I sucked in a breath, willing my hormones to take a chill pill. Just because he was here didn't mean he was staying.

Locking the door, I took a moment to collect myself, setting my stuff down by the door and pulling my boots off. My feet instantly felt better once they were free. Maddox wasn't right in the doorway, so I followed the sound and found him opening cabinets.

"Make yourself at home, why don't you?" I rolled my eyes, walking to the fridge.

"Thanks, I plan to."

I pulled out the water pitcher, walked to the cabinet with the glasses, and pulled two down. I filled them both and then put the pitcher back in the fridge.

Handing him one, I watched as he stopped opening drawers. I took a long drink of mine, the cold liquid soothing my dry throat and cooling me off inside.

"So, you're here. Talk."

I sat the glass down, crossing my arms. I didn't want to look at him too closely, but I couldn't help but notice how much bigger his muscles looked.

"Happy Birthday, Princess."

I sucked in a breath, not expecting him to say that. I looked at the clock on the stove and saw it read 12:01. He was right. It was my birthday. I was officially twenty-two years old.

"Thanks. You could've just sent a card, though."

He sat his glass down next to mine, walking toward me. My body instantly fell into the memory of him and relaxed, letting him close. Maddox cupped my jaw, and my body betrayed me by falling into his hand, sighing. Stupid, traitorous body.

"I've missed you, Princess."

I snorted, my eyes opening. "You have a funny way of showing it. I haven't even heard from you in months on the server. It's been hard enough without you being here, but then to ghost me completely." I shook my head, tears coming to my eyes. "I don't get you, Maddox. Why are you here? I can't have you coming and going from my life like this. It hurts too much."

He leaned forward, placing his forehead on mine. "I know, Princess. I know. I wish I was here to tell you I was back for good, but things haven't gone as I'd hoped."

"Will you tell me your plan or when you'll be back?"

"I can't." He tensed his jaw, biting back his words. "It's safer if you don't know."

My eyes hardened, and I gritted my teeth. "You're wrong." His eyes heated, his pupils going wide at the fire coursing through my veins. I gripped his shirt, pulling it between my hands. "I'm not the same girl you left at the motel. I'm not even the same girl who left Mississippi. And if you don't realize that soon, you're gonna miss out."

His hands moved to my hips, gripping me tightly. He moved closer, his bottom half-pressing into me as he towered over me. "Oh, Princess, I know. Why do you think I'm here? I couldn't stand to be apart from you a moment longer. If you don't think I haven't been watching everything you do, then you haven't been paying attention. My love for you wasn't conditional or even locational." He lifted me up, sitting me on the counter, stepping in between my legs. I sucked in a breath, sexual need riding me hard.

"That's not enough, though. I need more than just your pretty words, Maddox. I won't even bring up the fact you're practically stalking me." I rolled my eyes, trying to dispel my lust.

"What if I could give you tonight? If we had one night where the rest of the shit didn't matter, would that be enough for now?"

"I don't know."

He dipped his head, skating his nose against my neck, licking up to my ear. "Say, yes, Princess. Give us this one night where it's just you and me. I need it to survive."

I knew he meant his words to be seductive, but I heard the raw emotion, the pain, and it hit me that I wasn't being fair to him. I didn't know what he was doing or having to endure. It had been easier not to ask. Looking up into his eyes, I couldn't deny the love I saw there.

"Okay. One night. It will be enough for now."

As soon as I said yes, his lips fell to mine, and it was like time hadn't existed. His kiss was just as I remembered, and I found myself swept up into the passion between us. My legs wrapped around him, bringing his groin closer to me.

"Watching you dance in these tiny shorts was pure torture. I can't wait to slip beneath them." He bit my lip, pulling back. "But I don't want our first time to be on your kitchen counter. Hold on, Princess."

I wrapped my arms around him, tightening my legs as he carried me to my bedroom. Surprise flitted through me until I remembered what he said. I should feel creeped out by that, but part of me was used to Maddox being in the shadows, so it felt right.

He laid me on my bed, stopping only to pull his leather jacket and shirt off. He kicked off his boots and slid his pants down, crawling onto the bed in his boxers, hovering over me. His hands slid up my belly, pulling my shirt over my head. He stopped, taking me in with his eyes as he leaned back on his haunches.

"Yep, that's the image I want in my head forever.

You in this red lace bra and your cut-off shorts. Fuck, Darcie. That's a wet dream right there."

Leaning up, I slipped my straps off, borrowing some moves I'd learned. "Oh yeah? How about now?" I pulled my bra away, standing in front of him topless. Kneeling on the bed, I ran my hands up his torso, stopping when I spotted a tattoo on his chest. It was a crown with the letters DRC on it. I gasped, looking up. "Is that?"

He nodded, watching me. "It's how I have you with me always, never forgetting who owns my heart."

"Fuck." I wrapped my arms around his neck, needing to kiss him. "One night isn't ever going to be enough, Maddox." Tears were in my eyes as I stared at him. "I love you too, but it hurts."

"I know, Princess. We'll figure it out. Even if that means I have to let you go for a while, I will. I don't want to keep you caged. You're too beautiful for that. But for right now, let's just pretend."

I nodded, and he wiped the tears off my cheeks, kissing them away.

Things escalated quickly then. We fell to the bed, and our bottom halves rocked into one another. His fingers unbuttoned my shorts, pulling them off without breaking his kiss. Maddox kissed down my body, sucking my nipples into his mouth. My hands roamed his body, running outside his boxers, feeling him grow in my hand. Pushing the elastic down, I peeked down to see him fully.

Swallowing, I took him into my hand as he massaged and kissed my body. When I wrapped my hand around him, he stilled, taking a breath.

"Okay, new rule. This first time might be quick, but I said all night, so we pack as many times as we can into that. Sound good?"

I laughed, nodding. "That sounds like the best plan you've ever had."

He rolled on a condom, and I watched with heated eyes as he lined himself up with me. I felt the tip of his cock press into me, and he paused, looking at me. "Ready, Princess?"

I nodded, biting my lip. He bent down, kissing me as he pressed in. As he started to fill me, pain spread through me, and I gritted my teeth, breathing through it. Maddox kissed me harder, taking my mind off it.

"Almost there. You feel so good, Princess. Everything I ever dreamed it would be."

I tangled my fingers through the back of his hair, pulling his head to me, holding on. Once he stopped, I breathed, trying not to freak out. The pain reminded me too much of the other time, and I didn't like it.

"I need to feel good, Maddox. Please, make it feel good."

He pulled back, seeing my eyes, and nodded. "I got you." He started to rock forward, pulling back, and it got a little better each time. He pulled my leg up, pushing himself deeper. His thumb pressed against my clit, helping me not focus on the stretching. Each rock forward and pull backward led us to a rhythm, and I found myself moving with him. Soon, we were rocking together, and it felt better.

Maddox filled me fully, taking his time to feel all of me around him. His thumb on my button made my toes curl, and I found myself forgetting about the pain. "I need more," I whispered, hoping he'd understand.

He pulled back, gripping my hips, and began to thrust harder, pushing into me deeper.

"Yes, that," I moaned, the feeling increasing.

"Shit. I can't…" he stuttered, tensing as he held me. He looked down, shock on his face. "I'm sorry. It just felt too good, and it's my first time."

I reached up, rubbing his cheek. "It's okay, Maddox. We get all night, remember?"

He smiled, sighing in relief. "Yeah, we do. And while we wait for me to be ready, I'm going to take care of you."

He pulled out and walked into my bathroom,

disposing of the condom. I heard the water turn on and wondered what he was doing. He came back out with a washcloth. "I read that this might feel good."

Carefully, Maddox placed it on my lady parts, and the heat did feel nice. He cleaned me up, taking extra care to be gentle. When he was done, he pulled me into his arms, kissing me softly. His hands kept exploring, and he moved down, kissing me all over.

"I need to map out every inch of you."

"Feel free." I laughed, not minding at all. His fingers found their way to my core, and he quickly brought me the orgasm I'd been teetering around.

"Yes, yes," I screamed, my hands grasping at the sheets. Maddox kissed me, a smug look on his face, and I realized he was ready to go already. This time, he pulled me on top, and it didn't hurt as much. All night, we tried different positions, only stopping for food and water a couple of times. We went through a whole box of condoms, but it was everything I could've asked for.

Standing at the door, he held me in his arms, his lips on my forehead. "I don't want to leave."

"I don't want you to."

He kissed me one last time, pulling away. "Will I see you again?"

"Of course, Princess. This isn't goodbye forever."

"So until then, we just pretend like we didn't just fuck each other's brains out?"

"I'll never be able to pretend with you. This night has been the best one of my life, and it will be what gets me through the dark days ahead."

"I wish you'd just tell me. I don't know if I can do this again."

"We have to. You promised."

"I want to hate you. It's easier then."

"I know, Princess. I don't want you to wait, though. Keep living your life, and when it's our time, I'll come for you, and we'll ride off into the sunset. I promise."

"Fuck, I love you, Maddox. Don't make me miss you too much."

He kissed me hard, tears falling from both of our eyes as he stepped away and walked out that door.

I slid to the ground, not even making it a step before it felt like the world was falling apart again.

Dear Mom,

Have you ever felt so happy in one moment and broken in another? That's how it feels right now, with Maddox gone. Our night together was everything I knew it would be, but I miss him even more now. The loneliness isn't as consuming, though. Having friends has helped, and some of my clients I've gotten close to. It just sucks because I wish I could meet them in person.

It's kind of my life though—I can't have it all.

Every morning, I wake up and I promise myself I won't check the message board. I think I need some space from Maddox to heal. Not that I blame him, I don't. I understand

and I know what he's doing isn't easy, but it still hurts.

The thing I've noticed, though, I'm not as weak as I once was. It hurts to miss him, but I'm not lost anymore, and I'm really starting to like the Darcie I'm becoming.

Love you,

Darcie

Eleven

MADDOX

I tossed back another shot, hoping the burn would take the feel of her around me away. I thought if I had one night with Darcie, then I'd be able to focus, concentrate on the task ahead of me, and fight to make it back to her.

Instead, I was a pussy-whipped boy, unable to get her out of his head.

A slap on my back jolted me, and I tensed, not knowing who it was. I peeked out of the corner of my eye and spotted my father. Everything in me wanted to pull away, gut him, and ride off into the sunset back to my girl.

But that wasn't the plan. I was really starting to hate the plan.

Tank had been partially truthful to Darcie about the program. What he'd failed to mention was I'd been a part of the program from the very beginning, just not in any official capacity yet. It was my father who had sent me there to be a double agent in the first place, hoping to get one over Hank the Tank.

He hadn't taken into consideration I'd fallen in love with a girl and had an agenda of my own. When Hank had asked me why I wanted to be part of MCD, I'd told him flat out, surprising him. The memory of the conversation had been playing in my mind the past few months as I reminded myself of my goal and responsibility.

"Why do you want to be part of the Mavericks, Son?"

I gritted my teeth, biting back the words. "My father sent me here to learn your secrets and to use them against you so he can take over your club someday. He doesn't trust you and wants in on whatever foothold you seem to have gained."

He watched me, a careful look on his face. "I'll ask it again. Why do you want to be part of MCD?"

I relaxed, respecting the man I'd always watched from the shadows when we'd visit. "I want to become the best, so I can kill my father and take over his reign."

"While I admire your ambition, what would make you a better leader? I don't condone patricide."

"My father is a murderer, thief, and a liar. He sold my mother off to another club when he was in debt. He

doesn't protect those in his club and demands blind loyalty. He's a vile dictator who only wants power and control. He doesn't care about anyone or anything. I've seen what you can do here, I know your club is different, and I want that type of place. I love to ride, and I know it's a life I'll lead, but I just don't want to do it under him."

"Why not join another club then? Why kill your father and take over?"

"Because it's never that simple, is it?" I asked, keeping my gaze steady. Sucking in a breath, I took a chance and told Hank my secrets. "One, I'm in love with your daughter, have been ever since I knew what girls were."

He chuckled, giving me a different look over now. "And two?"

"I have a special needs sister. She's away at school now, but one day she'll return, and when she does, I want it to be a safe place."

Hank cupped his jaw regarding me. "If you pass the program, then I'll read you into what's really going on here. As for my daughter, you'll have to win her heart on your own."

"How was your trip? Did you make contact with a buyer?"

I nodded, taking the last shot and turning to deal

with my father. Now that I was older, I was as big as him, possibly even bigger.

"He's agreed to the arrangement and will be ready for you at the end of the month."

"Good, good. Come, I have a present for you."

He smiled wide, not building a lot of confidence in me that I'd like this present. I'd been able to arrange the meeting to coincide with Darcie's birthday. I hadn't planned on sleeping with her, but it was the only thing on my mind once I was there.

Especially after watching her online for months.

I'd been heartbroken at first when I saw what she was doing, but then I realized why. I knew she needed to find her own footing in her sexuality, and with me leaving, she didn't have someone to help cover bills. She was surviving and healing, and it was all I wanted for her. I couldn't be mad at her for finding her own way.

So, I sucked it up and watched and discovered a whole new reason to love her. Darcie was blossoming, and I couldn't deny her the space to do that, even if it hurt to think she could forget me. She didn't know I was there, but I never missed a video, and it allowed me to help her without her knowing. It kept me in her world in a safe way.

Walking through the dusty club, I nodded at a few other members, but mostly, I kept my focus on the man next to me. Destroyer wasn't one for words, so I walked silently next to him, calculating all the different things he could have for me.

When I stepped into my room, I stopped, frozen in my tracks. It wasn't uncommon to see naked women in the clubhouse, many of them sweet butts hoping to score or become an old lady.

But the two young females lying on my bed, kissing and touching one another, weren't what I expected. I swallowed, turning to my father. "I don't understand."

He laughed. "Fuck, Maddox. I thought you were shy, but you do know what pussy is, right? Please tell me you're not a virgin? Did Tank not have any prime-grade sweet butts for you to fuck while you were there?"

"I'm not a virgin," I said, ignoring the rest. At least now when I said that it was true. My father had been on me to taste the products more recently, but I never expected him to go out of his way by shoving two naked teens at me. Not that I was a lot older at 24, but they barely looked 18. "Why are you giving me girls?" I asked, turning to him. "I'm capable of finding my own."

"I thought you could use a distraction from your girl now that you're here to stay. And after your trip,

I wanted to reward you. But if you don't want my gift, then I'll just give them to the guys."

I swallowed, not wanting to subject these girls to the assholes he called brothers. "No, it's fine. Can I have some privacy then?"

"There's my boy." He clapped me on the back, walking out of the room. "Come see me when you're done. There's some business I need to discuss. I've found a match for your sister." He grinned wide, his burden finally off his plate in his eyes.

Gritting my teeth, I nodded, watching him walk out of the room. The door clicking allowed me to relax, some of the tension leaving the room with him gone. Hands touched me from behind, and I jumped, spinning.

"No," I said, pointing.

"But you said…" she pouted.

Shielding my eyes, I walked over to where I spotted their clothes. "It doesn't matter what I said. I'm saying no. Please, get dressed. I won't be having sex with you."

"Then what are we doing?" the other asked, not wasting time to put her clothes on. Smart girl.

"I don't know. You can't leave for a bit, so he'll think we had sex. We could watch a movie or play video games, I guess."

In my mind, it was the furthest thing I wanted to

do, but I knew I had to weigh everything precisely right now. If he was already moving forward with his plan for Becca, then I had to think fast.

The girls settled on the couch with snacks and pulled up a movie. I pulled out my computer, checking all my accounts and seeing if there were any new messages from Tank. I knew he was avoiding Darcie, but he'd been talking with me after I told him the update on the situation. He was mad at first that I'd left her, but when I'd told him what was at stake, he eventually agreed it had been the right call.

If I'd gone to jail then, not only would that have left Darcie vulnerable, but Becca too, and the whole operation we had against my father would've fallen apart. I only needed a few more pieces of evidence, and we could put him away.

No, I had to go home, even if it was the last thing I'd wanted to do at the time.

There weren't any new messages on the server, but I did have a new message from a contact. Pulling it up, I glanced over at the girls, but they were still immersed in the movie.

MadDog,
I got what you need. Let's meet tonight.
Tom

A sigh of relief filled me, and I relaxed back into the couch. A ping went off, and I looked at my notifications, finding a new message from Rose.

Liquid heat surged forward, and I wished the girls were gone now. Clicking on the message, I scanned it quickly, devouring every word.

Shadow,

How's your week been? Did the project you've been working on finish? Things have been up and down for me. I turned another year older and got a visit from an old friend. It was nice. It's just so hard to say goodbye. I've had to do that a lot in my life.

You were talking about motorcycles in your last message. What kind do you have? I'm thinking of getting one for myself. I miss riding.

Hope you're having a fantastic day. Let's meet up in the private chat again, soon.

Rose

She missed me.

It shouldn't feel as good as it did. I knew it was hurting her, but it gave me hope, and that was what I needed to keep pushing through.

When the movie ended, I helped the girls get off the property without running into any other members. I didn't know where my father found them or what he promised them, but I didn't want to put any other girls in the position Darcie had been. The last thing I wanted was for them to be subjected to that.

I had a few hours before I needed to meet Tom, so I veered toward Becca's room, wanting to check in with her since I'd been gone. Nodding at the guard permanently stationed at her door, I knocked on the hot pink monstrosity and waited until I heard her shout I could enter.

"Bubbie!" she yelled, jumping off the bed and running toward me. I held her tight, always enjoying Becca's hugs.

"Hey, squirt. How's my favorite girl?"

She laughed. "I'm not your favorite. Darcie is."

"You can both be my favorite. Whatcha working on?" I leaned against her desk as she settled back on the floor next to a coloring book. Becca was twenty and had Down Syndrome. She'd been at a school for most of the year, letting her have some space from the club. I didn't respect my father, but he'd at least given her a chance to have an everyday life. Though, his reasons were to make her more attractive to a suitor and hope to keep her pure if she wasn't around feral men all the time.

I hadn't cared too much about his reasons, as long as it kept her safer. But now that she'd graduated, he was moving up his plans to send her off. I couldn't let that happen. I'd been working with the Mavericks to get her into hiding if necessary. But ultimately, I was working on setting up a different meet where my father thought she was sold, but it was to someone safe. I knew if he didn't get something from the exchange, he wouldn't stop looking for her. Meeting with Tom, I hoped to finally have a viable option. It was needed now more than ever.

"I'm making a picture to take to my new home."

"Your new home?" I asked, fear filling me.

"Yeah, Daddy said I was going to meet my husband."

Becca's innocence was too pure for someone to tarnish.

"Oh, how are you feeling about that?"

She shrugged. "If he buys me a puppy, I'll be happy."

I smiled, knowing how much she'd wanted a pet her whole life. "Hmm, is that so? Well, I just wanted to come and give my best girl a hug. I have some things to do, but I'll see you later. Do not leave until you say bye, okay?"

"Okay." She stood, giving me another hug.

"Love you, Bubbie."

"Love you too, Squirt."

When the time to meet Tom rolled around, I snuck out, hoping my father wouldn't come and check on me. Except, it seemed like he'd had an ace up his sleeve and had been testing me.

"Hands up where we can see them!" the officer yelled as he and his colleagues stormed the place I'd been waiting. Dread filled me, knowing I'd been set up, and it was time to pull my emergency card.

"Maddox King, you're under arrest for drug trafficking. You have the right to remain silent…"

"I'd like to make my one phone call."

"You can do that at the station."

"No, I need to do it now. *Songbird.*"

The police officer's eyes widened, but he nodded, un-cuffed me, and handed me his cell phone.

I dialed the number, the phone ringing a few times before someone answered. I didn't waste time, knowing every second from here counted.

"I'd like to call in my favor."

"It's done."

"Thank you."

"You know what this means, though, right, Maddox?"

"Yes. I'm aware. I have to, though. Becca needs you more."

"It will be done within the hour. Good luck on the inside."

"Thanks. Don't tell Darcie."

"She'll hate you for this."

"It's better this way," I said.

He sighed, and I knew he was weighing his words. "I wish it could be different. I have the information you sent. I'll try to get you out quickly."

"I know. But we both know how these things work. If Becca's safe, I'll wait as long as I have to."

"You have my word."

I hung up. Nothing else needed to be said, and handed the phone back to the officer. He cuffed me again but was more gentle this time.

Every officer from Alabama to Mississippi to Georgia knew what those words meant. But once I was on the inside, I was on my own.

I only hoped Darcie wouldn't forget me.

Diary #11

Dear Mom,

I know something has gone wrong with Maddox's mission. While we didn't talk every day on the server, we checked in with one another. I haven't heard from him in a month now, and I'm worried.

But I know he wouldn't want me to be. So, I'm trying to go about my days, living my life here in Nashville.

I can't believe I've lived in the city for a year now. Life is going well, and history makes me nervous, but I'm trying not to let that stop me from living it.

Speaking of, I've let Candi set me up on a date.

I'm a little nervous, but I think it's time, as

hard as that is to admit. I'm not giving up on Maddox, but I can't wait and he told me not to.

Dad still hasn't responded, but I know he's seeing them, and that's enough for now.

Love you,

Darcie

<h1 style="text-align:center">Twelve</h1>

DARCIE

Blotting my lips, I smacked them together as I finished with my lipstick. Cherry red tonight. I was ready to dance and flirt with all the boys. My confidence had soared since I became a cam girl. Self assurance wasn't something I'd ever thought I'd need, having always been confident in who I was before Agonizer stole it.

Reclaiming it through the camera was one of the things that saved me. I knew my body now in ways I'd never known it before. I knew what I liked about myself and, most importantly, I felt ready to explore it with real partners now.

My sex drive had increased tenfold as well, and I was ready to cross that bridge. Somewhere in my mind, I think I hoped Maddox would show up again and stop me, lurking in the shadows as he did, even though a more significant part of me knew he wasn't here, something keeping him from me this time.

My phone vibrated as I locked up, and I jogged down the steps as best as I could in cowboy boots. One day I'd learn to wear better footwear, but tonight wasn't that night. I was going with girlie today in a simple pink dress and brown boots. The dress was thin, helping me not die in the summer heat.

Stepping out into the sun, I waved at Candi as I hurried to her car. We were headed to an outdoor country music festival she'd snagged us tickets to.

"Hey, girlfriend!" she said, smiling over at me.

"Hey! You look great! I love your look." She had on a denim skirt and a gingham style shirt she'd tied at the waist, along with hot pink cowboy boots and a matching hat.

"I'm hoping to snag me a cowboy! Howdy!" Candi exclaimed, making a roping motion with her arm.

"As long as he's hot, I don't care what he does."

Laughing, we took off, cranking up the radio as we sang along to it. When I thought about the girl I was a year and a half ago, I didn't even recognize myself, and for that, I was glad.

"So, you're gonna do it, huh?" she asked, pulling into the field we were directed to park in.

"Hook up?" I asked.

"Yeah. I know you don't normally do it."

"I'm ready." I hadn't told Candi all of my history, but she'd picked up things from observation.

"I'm happy for you, Darce. Bout time you got laid."

"Hey! I was making sure I was ready, and now, I'm ready."

"As your good friend, then I must help you find the perfect guy to bone."

"Bone? What, are you eight?" We got out of the car, laughing as we began the trek toward the music. Linking arms together, we followed the others, looking around at everyone.

"Oh, what about that one?" she said, pointing at a blond guy.

"Eh, too skinny."

"Okay, what about that one?"

I shook my head immediately. "No, too frat boy."

"Ugh. Too picky. What's your type then?"

"Hmm, well, I do have a thing for guys on motor-cycles. Tattoos. Muscles."

"Ooooh, Darcie likes the bad boys."

"I do not!" I slapped her, laughing. Though, maybe I did.

"If he's just to mess around with, though, I guess he just needs to not smell, have his teeth, and be bigger than me. I don't want a guy who I'll feel like will break if he tries to pick me up."

"You want a man that can throw you around, huh?"

Giggling, I shrugged. I hadn't meant to describe Maddox, but she had a point. I kind of did like that.

We showed our tickets on our phones, and they gave us wrist bracelets, dictating what sections we could get into. Candi's connection had gotten us VIP tickets, giving us special admittance. Most of the groups playing I wasn't familiar with, but live music was always fun, and I was excited to hear all that was on offer.

Together, we headed back to the area her friend was in. Candi pointed out guys along the way she thought I might want to bone. Every time she said bone, I'd bust out laughing, shaking my head, and the guy would look at me like I was deranged. Some wing-woman she was.

Showing our bracelets to a bouncer, we were let back into a smaller section. "Come on, I want you to meet some people."

A group of guys were gathered around some couches set up under the tent. Huge industrial fans blew, but it wasn't necessarily any cooler. The humid air just moved more. As we approached, a guy caught my eye, and I stopped, looking him over. Candi nudged me, waggling her eyebrows.

"Oh, you got the look. Which one is he?"

"What are you talking about?" I said, trying to play dumb.

"Don't you do that with me! Tell me, or I'll shout to the whole tent you're open for business."

Gasping, I pinched her arm. "You wouldn't dare."

She crossed her arms. "Try me." Raising an eyebrow, she waited me out. Sighing, I pulled her close, giving in.

"Fine, he's the one with the dark hair, sleeve of tattoos, and has the Waylon Jennings shirt on," I mumbled, a blush rising to my cheeks.

"See, you do like a bad boy." She giggled, getting delighted in my embarrassment.

"Why are we friends?" I asked, crossing my arms.

"Because I'm fabulous," she said, tossing her hair over her shoulder. "And I know who that is. So, I can give you an introduction. Now, who's salty?"

Dropping my arms, I smiled, giving her a hug. "Okay, fine. You win. So, what do you know?" I asked, finding myself with a crush.

"His name's Damon, and he works at Wild Horse as a bartender. He's kind of on the loner side, though. I don't see him around too much. His brother is the lead singer of the band."

"Ah, well, he sounds kind of like a douche, then."

"Hey, it's your type. I just tell it how it is."

"Fine. You might also have a point. Okay, I'm going in."

Using everything I'd learned, I walked over, feeling confident. "Hi, I'm Darcie."

He glanced up, running his eyes over my body, and then took a drink, looking at me. "Not interested." After that, he turned and walked off. I stood there for a solid minute, trying to figure out what had just happened.

"Um, what?"

Another guy walked up, placing his arm around me. "Don't worry about him. He's an ass to everyone. I'm the much nicer and cooler brother. I'm Stefan," he said, peering down at me.

"Wait, like the Salvatore brothers?" I asked, looking into his eyes.

He rolled them but nodded. "Yep. Our mother was a huge fan of the books before they became a TV show. And like the characters, I'm the nice and friendly one."

"It's nice to meet you, Stefan. I'm Darcie."

"Well, it's my lucky day because the prettiest girl here is talking to me."

"Okay, sweet talker, got anything to back up those

words?" I raised my eyebrow, and I realized I was flirting with him. It had come naturally, and I knew I'd been right. I was ready for this.

"As a matter of fact," he leaned in, boldly kissing me, taking me by surprise. It wasn't a horrible kiss, so I leaned into it, rising up on my toes. When he pulled back, he grinned.

"Care to be my date for the day, Darcie?"

"Sounds fun."

And it was. I hung out with the band and Stefan until they had to perform. Damon stayed clear of us, keeping to himself as he read a book in a corner. Candi seemed to have met twin brothers, and I wasn't sure which one she liked more or if she cared.

That time of night was coming when I knew he would ask me to hook up, and I was ready.

"So, Darcie, would you like to go to the afterparty with me?"

"I'd love to."

"Cool. Let's go." He grinned wide, pulling me along, his hand in mine. I felt like every other girl in the world who'd met a guy and was going to go home with him. I could do this. This was normal. When we got to his truck, he pressed me up against the side of it, kissing me again.

If I didn't think about him, I could enjoy it. It felt

good, and I liked the way his hands traveled my body. He just wasn't someone I wanted to spend more time with outside this moment.

"Second thought, what if we head to the RV and skip the party?" he asked, his voice taking on a husky quality.

"Okay. Um, do you have a condom?" I asked.

"Yeah, yeah, we're good."

He pulled me along to a different section where RVs and campers had parked, weaving his way through them with ease.

"So, do you do this often? Hook up with girls at shows?" I asked.

"Sometimes. Kind of a perk, I guess." He shrugged, throwing me his million-dollar smile.

"Yeah, sure."

He opened up the door and motioned for me to enter. The space was clean, and I felt better about my decision. Stefan pulled me to the back and locked the door. Immediately, he started kissing me again, and I closed my eyes to get back to the place we'd been.

His calloused hand squeezed my breast, and I moved it away, not liking his touch. He managed to get my dress off, and I sat back on the bed, Rose kicking in.

"So, tell me," I asked, unbuckling his belt. "What do you want in a girl?"

His pupils dilated, and he licked his lips. "What do you mean?"

"I can be whoever you want me to be." I pulled his pants down and was shocked at his dick. It wasn't small, but I'd gotten used to Cowboy's and Maddox's, I guess, expecting more. Stroking it, he groaned, nodding, so I kept going.

"That, I like that." He reached around to a drawer, climbing onto the bed, and I watched as he rolled on the condom. It wasn't as sexy when he did it.

He kissed me again, his hands roaming me, and I pretended it was someone else. The conversation I had with Cowboy last night came to mind.

"I want to trace every inch of you, Rose. If I could, I'd spend all day learning how you liked to be touched. I'd give you so many orgasms, you wouldn't be able to walk for a week."

"I think that would be from your cock," I teased. Watching as he stroked his massive erection.

"You probably hear this all the time, but I think about you a lot."

"You do?" I asked, my breath hitching.

"Yeah. I, uh, I even imagine you when I'm talking to other girls. It's the only way I can…"

"Oh? And how do things go with them?" I asked, touching myself as I watched him.

"It just depends. Sometimes, it's harder to pretend than others."

"What do you mean?"

"There's only one Rose, and they're not it. But since I can't have you, I make do."

"Well, right here, it's just us. So, let's pretend we're together. Tell me what you'd do."

"Once you'd cum on my fingers multiple times, then I'd cover you with kisses. I want you good and ready for me, Rose. Because I know the moment I slide into you, I'm a goner."

The feeling of something pressing into me pulled me from my fantasy, and I realized Stefan was already heading to home plate. So much for foreplay.

He pushed in, grunting as he thrust, his dick hitting me in a pleasant way. I tried to imagine he was someone I liked, or at least focused on the pleasure, but he was so focused on thrusting, his breaths hitting my neck, it was hard to fall back into the fantasy. So, I decided I'd go after my own pleasure.

Reaching my hand down, I flicked my clit, rubbing it quickly to bring me back to that place I'd been before he'd begun to hump me.

Squeezing my eyes tight, I focused on my hand and how it felt when I was alone, watching Cowboy stroke his big dick. Stefan jerked in me, sputtering, and I somehow managed to find my own release, picturing the massive cum shot Cowboy had last night.

"So, good, Cowboy," I slurred.

Stefan chuckled, and I realized my mistake, but thankfully, he played it off as a nickname.

"You weren't too bad yourself, doll. Do you need a lift home?" he asked, pulling out and rolling over.

"Oh, yeah, let me check with my friend." I sat up, and reached to grab my dress, pulling it over. I didn't want to be naked around him anymore, feeling too vulnerable.

ME: Are you still here?

I waited a few minutes but didn't get a response. Looking up, I nodded to Stefan. "Yeah, looks like I could use a ride. Thanks."

"No, problem. Damon?" he shouted, and I almost screamed when the door opened, his brother appearing. He ignored me, glancing at Stefan.

"What?"

"Can you give Darcie a ride home? I've had a few and need to get some sleep before tomorrow's show." Damon gritted his teeth, and I opened my mouth to say I'd find another one when he looked at me.

"Yeah, sure. Come on. I'm not waiting all night."

I scooped up my stuff and waved at Stefan, who was already getting himself ready for bed. He didn't even acknowledge me as I passed him. I was suddenly rethinking his comment about being the nice brother.

Damon led me back to the truck we'd stopped at earlier, not saying a word the whole time. It was awkward, but since I didn't have a lot of options out in the country, I wasn't going to complain.

When we pulled into the city, I gave him directions to my apartment.

"Candi mentioned you worked at Wild Horse. I like it there."

"Yep," he said.

"Do you like working there?" I asked, the quiet getting to me.

"Yep."

"Do you often have to drive your brother's booty calls?"

"Yep."

"Do you know any other words?" I teased.

He stopped, a small smile threatening to take over his face. "Yep."

Laughing, I decided he wasn't too horrible, even if he wasn't the greatest conversationalist.

"He's not going to call you, you know." He finally said as we pulled up to my place.

"I know. I don't want him to."

That seemed to stun him, and he looked at me. "That's a first. Most girls think their vagina will make him fall in love with them."

"First of all, I'm pretty sure my vagina would. But second, his dick, not so much. He didn't even know how to do any foreplay. He gets by on his good looks and charm and the fact he's a somewhat star. It was good for tonight, but you don't have to worry about me becoming a stalker. "

Damon laughed, catching me off guard. "Okay, I think that's the first time any girl has ever referred to my brother as mediocre."

I shrugged, opening the door. "Thanks for the lift. You're not so scary, either."

He humphed, shaking his head. Closing the door, I walked a few steps when the window rolled down, and he called out to me.

"Hey!"

"Yeah?" I asked, turning.

"We're hiring, at Wild Horse, if you have any dance skills, you should apply. I won't say I know you, though. You're on your own."

"Thanks, I think."

He rolled his eyes, rolling up the window, but I caught a slight glimpse of a smile. Walking into the building, I deemed the night a moderate success. I'd had sex. It hadn't been great, but I hadn't ended up crying in the corner either. And I might be able to get a dream job. All in all, a red banner day.

Diary #12

Dear Mom,

Another year has passed, and I sometimes don't recognize my life before Nashville. It feels like a dream at times. I know I haven't even written as much either. I guess in some ways, that's good. I don't need to heal as much anymore. I miss sharing things with you, though.

So, how about an update?

I love my job at the Wild Horse Saloon. It took me six months to earn a spot as a dance instructor, but I never gave up, taking more classes so I could learn the steps to all of them. Damon still avoids me, but he'll talk to me every now and then. I think it helps that I wasn't hung up on Stefan like he expected.

Though getting promoted has hampered things, and he's gone back to hating me, I think.

My sexual experiences have been better since Stefan. No one has been Maddox, but I'm guessing that's because we loved one another. I try not to think about him, but I know something terrible happened. I just hope that one day he'll be able to tell me about it. I refuse to think he's gone.

Candi is as crazy as ever, and she's been a real friend. Even when there was an incident over a guy with some of her other friends, she stood by me. I didn't know he had a girlfriend, but you'd think I waltzed in there and demanded he perform mediocre oral on me. Based on his limp dick, I'm guessing Valerie owns his balls as it was. It taught me to pick guys who were clearly single and not hanging around our group.

Candi asked if I had ever thought about getting a boyfriend. She's currently shacked up with someone and is all lovesick. I'll admit, I'm still a hopeless romantic and daydream of someone making a romantic gesture one day. But I'm not there yet. Or maybe just the right person hasn't come along. Hookups are just easier. No emotions involved.

Besides, my heart is already wrapped up in a few people. *Yeah, a few.*

I should feel bad, but I don't. For one, none of them are attainable. So, if they're all just in my heart, what's the harm?

Maddox is a permanent fixture. I'll never stop loving him.

Cowboy has become my best friend, and if we ever met, I'd probably run off to Gatlinburg and get married in a drive-up wedding chapel. He's pure and wholesome, despite most of our conversations being naked.

Chase is a mystery, but he's still in my life. The schoolgirl crush I had on him still activates when he texts. I know we can't be together, and I don't even know if I do like him since it's been over two years since I've even seen him, but I think about the what-ifs sometimes. He's been a good friend to me, helping me when I needed it. It's too complicated, though, for me to settle down with anyone else.

At least, that's my reasoning. I guess, in a way, Damon fits that too. Maybe I just like guys who didn't or couldn't be with me so I wouldn't get hurt.

Wow, that was dark.

Moving on. I've decided to get a tattoo. My appointment is tonight, and I'm excited about it. I guess that's all.

Love,

Darcie

Thirteen

DARCIE

I walked into the tattoo parlor and immediately loved it. The atmosphere had a fun and hip vibe, making me trust their work. I was already in love with all the designs I'd seen on LiveIt.

A guy sat at the front counter reading, so I walked up to him with confidence, smiling big as I braced my arms against the counter. "Hi, I'm here for an appointment."

"Name?" he asked in a bored tone, not looking up.

"Darcie."

"Right. You're with one of our new artists, LJ. Can you sign this waiver?" He handed me a clipboard, still more focused on his book.

"Why do I have to sign a waiver? Are they not

good?" He rolled his eyes, and I wanted to throat punch the jerk.

Leaning forward more, I pressed my boobs together. He instantly dropped his eyes, gulping. Stroking the arm holding out the form, I finally managed to get his attention.

"Um, what did you say?" he asked, swallowing.

"Why do I have to sign a waiver? It won't hurt, will it?" I purred.

"It's for liability, not the artist. She's actually one of our best. And um, it might hurt. Is that a problem?"

I stroked my finger up and down, looking up through my eyelashes. "A little pain can be good," I said, using my best bedroom voice. He gulped again, nodding so fast he looked like a bobble-head. He eventually got enough courage to lean closer.

"So, hey, I get off in a few if you want to grab a drink after."

I pouted. "I don't know. I'm not really interested in a threesome with your phone. Good luck with that."

A girl had walked up while I'd been talking and stood back watching. She laughed when she heard what I said, and I looked over, smiling at her.

"Please tell me that you're my client?" she asked, grinning.

"Um, she is LJ," the guy said, blushing. "She needs to sign the waiver."

I grabbed it, signed it quickly, and handed it back. Walking over to her, I grabbed her arm, and she led me to a room. "So, I wanted a tattoo, but your piercings are fabulous. So, now, I'm not sure."

"Why choose?" she said, smiling.

"I like how you think. Yes! Let's do it." She giggled, showing me where to sit.

"I'm LJ. What did you have in mind today?" She sat on a stool, scooting closer.

"I want a rose, but like a badass rose."

"Okay, and where would you like this badass rose."

"See, I like you. You don't question it. Hmm?" I tapped my chin. "I've been debating, actually. Shoulder blade or my pelvic bone."

LJ pulled out a pad of paper, beginning to draw as she asked questions. "How big do you want it? Do you want thorns or just the bloom?"

"Just the bloom, and I'm open to suggestions. This is my first. Where did you get yours?"

She paused, looking up. "Oh, well, I don't have a tattoo yet."

"What! Okay, there has to be a story there. I've got all the time in the world, so how about you tell me."

"You're kind of pushy, you know." She bit her lip,

and I braced my head on my hand, giving her my best puppy dog eyes, hoping they worked on girls too. "Fine," she sighed, smiling. "Last question before I tell you my sordid tale."

"Oh, now this sounds juicy. And hit me with it, girl."

"Are you wanting your tattoo for yourself or to show it off to others?"

"Hmm, that's a good point. I think for myself."

"Then smaller on your pelvic bone is my suggestion."

I nodded, agreeing. "I like it. Okay, spill."

She started to sketch more but started to talk. "It happens to involve a guy."

"Of course," I said, nodding. "The best stories always do."

She smiled, the pen a soothing sound as it brushed against the paper. She flipped it over, showing me. "Okay, that's perfect. Are you in my mind or something?" LJ shrugged, blushing a little. "So, this boy?"

She giggled, the sound light, and I liked it. "We met as pen pals. He wanted to be a tattoo artist and said he'd give me my first one. He even drew one he designed for me. It was beautiful."

"I don't understand. Why don't you have it then?"

She pulled out her equipment, motioning for me to lay down and unzip my jeans. "He lived on the west coast, and I lived north of here. I was, um, getting serious with someone and told him I couldn't be his pen pal anymore."

"Wait, how long did you guys write?"

"Around eight years."

"Holy shit! Did you have feelings for him?"

"I mean, yeah. I was fifteen when I started writing to him, and I fell in love with him over the years from writing to each other. But in the end, it didn't matter. He wasn't who he said he was, and then I lost the only guy I cared about."

"Whoa, that went dark fast."

Her shoulder tensed. "That's just the past few years; that's not even the past few months," she mumbled.

"My ears are ready to listen," I said, hoping she'd take it as an invitation. Her eyes held shadows like mine, and I recognized the heartbreak in them. This girl and I were kindred spirits.

"You sure you want to hear this?" she asked, looking up.

I nodded, smiling softly at her. "Yep. You and me, I can tell we're gonna be friends. Might as well use this time to get to know all the baggage."

She laughed, smiling. "Okay, you asked for it."

Over the next hour as she tattooed me, she told me the story of Simon and Slade, and how she'd ended up in Nashville.

"That settles it," I said. "You're coming out with me dancing. It's the best cure for heartbreak."

"Hmm, I don't know."

"Come on, bestie. I promise you will enjoy it. I just so happen to know the perfect place."

"Fine," she rolled her eyes but smiled. "And you're done."

I looked down in awe at the rose she'd drawn. "I love it. Thank you."

"Of course. Still wanting that piercing?"

"Yes, but I think I'll hold off on it for today. That way, I have another excuse to come and visit you, LJ."

"It's Lennox, actually. I just use LJ here, but I prefer Lennox."

"You got it. It suits you better. So, where do you live?" I asked.

"Here."

"Ha, ha. Don't we all live at work? But really." I lifted an eyebrow, telling her to spill.

"No, really. I live upstairs. I'll have Ethan finish your care, and I'll go change. Thankfully, you're my last client, so I'm free. Just come up the back stairs if I'm not done."

"Sounds like a plan."

She walked out, giving instructions to the guy who'd ignored me earlier. He was all red as he put ointment on me and wrapped it. I didn't care; I was more excited about making a friend on my own.

Lennox came down a few minutes later, and we headed over to the Wild Horse Saloon. When we walked in, I saw Damon was at the bar, and I rolled my eyes. We'd gotten into it the other day over me being a manager. It was my job to make the schedule now, and he didn't like one of the days I'd given him, stating it was an agreement with the last manager he had that day off. He refused to tell me why, so I said he'd have to work it.

He called in sick, pissing me off even more. We were now in a brutal battle for dominance. He pushed my buttons, and I refused to give in. It was only a matter of time now before one of us folded. I was holding out that it would be him.

"Who's that?" Lennox asked, noticing the hate-filled eye war we had going on.

"Damon. The bane of my existence."

"Hmm, sounds like there's more to this story."

"Nope. Come on, we can go to a different bartender." I pulled her along, ignoring the hot guy at the other end. Tonight was about new friendships, and I was here to dance. Bad boys and their attitudes could stay far away.

"Okay, this has been a blast. We must do it again," Lennox said as she downed a bottle of water a few hours later.

"Yay! I feel like we're going to be best friends. Give me your number, and we can hang out more."

"Sure." She handed me her phone, and I put in my number, texting myself.

"Come on, I'll walk you home. You're on my way. We actually live pretty close to one another."

"Really? That's awesome. Thanks for talking me into this. I didn't realize how much I needed to get out of my comfort zone. Oh, hey, look, there's Thane. Come and say hello."

We walked over to a tall guy with blonde hair. He was model attractive, but something about him didn't do it for me. He hugged Lennox with a possessive glint in his eye, and I wondered if she knew he harbored feelings for her. Interesting new development.

"Thane, this is my new bestie, Darcie."

"Howdy." I waved, smiling friendly.

"Nice to meet you," he said quickly, dropping his eyes back to Lennox. "Can I walk you home?"

"Oh," she looked at me, and I waved her off.

"It's fine. I can make it to my place. I do this trek almost every night. But text me, and we'll grab lunch."

She pulled me in for a hug, squeezing me tight. Lennox was a great hugger. "Don't forget to take care of your tattoo." She pulled back, winking.

"Right. Laters."

They walked off toward the tattoo parlor. I didn't want it to seem like I was following them since I had to go in the same direction, so I stood in line to grab some food to take back. Once I had it with me, I started on my journey home, realizing how lonely it felt now. I'd done this a million times, but for some reason, it felt different tonight.

Pulling out my phone, I scrolled through messages. Candi had never showed up, and I wondered what had happened. When I saw the missed messages, my stomach dropped.

Candi: Shit. Darcie. Something terrible is going down. You haven't had any personal relationships, right?

Candi: That bitch Lucinda busted me, and now they're going through the whole server.

Candi: I'm sorry I didn't tell you that my new sugar daddy was from the site. I thought it would keep you safe.

Candi: I'm locked out. What am I going to do? They've disabled my account and are holding my funds for this month. I have rent to pay. John's not going to be happy about this. I'm spiraling.

Candi: Darcie! Call me back asap. I might have a solution.

I hit call on her contact, but it went to voicemail. "Hey, it's me. Call me back."

I clicked on my email and saw I had new messages from the server. Shit! Looked like they'd locked me out, too. But I thought I'd been careful? I'd never met anyone outside of the chat rooms. Yes, things had gotten personal, but I didn't know that was wrong.

Fuck. Cowboy would think I'd left. I didn't know how to get a hold of him, and with Candi locked out too, there wasn't anyone for me to have reach out to him.

Maybe I could make a fake account? No, that wouldn't work. I had to provide all of my information to get paid. Shit. Shit. Shit.

My apartment building came into view, and I

hurriedly rushed up the stairs. My food was in one hand, my keys in the other as I beelined for my door. If I could check online, then I'd know. I could try to get some answers before it was too late.

My phone started ringing, and I went to reach for it, my food creating a barrier to grab it. Pulling it out, I raised it to my ear to answer. "Hello?"

"Darcie. Shit. Have you gotten on? Did they get you too?"

"I don't know. I'm just getting home. How did this happen?" I asked, juggling my stuff to open the door. Once inside, I tossed everything onto the counter and opened my computer. I set the phone down, pushing the speaker button.

"Candi, I can't get in either. Shit. What do we do now?"

"I don't know. I'm so sorry, Darcie."

"It's not your fault," I said, trying not to panic.

"It kind of feels like it. I violated the rule. I fell in love with a client." She started sobbing, and I soothed her with nonsensical words, but all I could think was I'd never get to talk to Cowboy again.

Diary #13

Dear Mom,
    Everything is shit.
    Love,
    Darcie

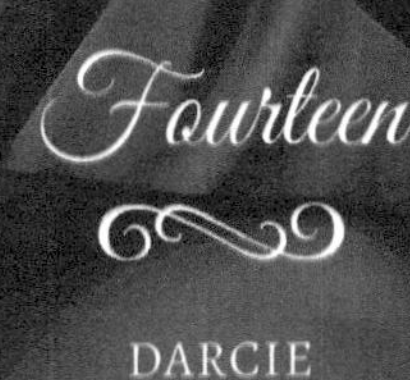

Fourteen

DARCIE

Without the website to fall back on, I had to start picking up more shifts at the bar. Thankfully, I made more money as a manager, and I'd saved a lot over the years, but I'd also spent a lot. A girl and her shoes were sacred.

The official story was that the site had been hacked by a jealous lover and reported to the FBI that underage girls were there. While they were investigating, everyone was shut down as they combed through all the videos and messages. It made me feel violated in a way I'd never considered before. It was fine when it was people talking to me, but random men and women viewing things out of context felt a lot like someone reading my diary.

While I did miss the money, I missed Shadow and

Cowboy more, even if I hadn't heard from Shadow in a while. I wished I'd thought of some contingency plan on how to connect, but I never thought this would happen, and my dad would say that was my first mistake. *"Always know your escape plan and be prepared for it all to go to shit."*

Needless to say, I'd be doing that from now on. It seemed even when I guarded my heart, I was still capable of being hurt.

"What's crawled up your butt?" Damon asked, eyeing me.

"Eww, and nothing."

He watched me, not buying my lie. "You've been a downer for a month straight. What gives? Your boyfriend dump you? Did you get herpes? Your favorite boy band break up?"

Scrunching up my nose, I stuck my tongue out at him. We'd officially moved into enemy territory now. "Why would I tell you? You'll just use it for ammo."

He sighed, rubbing his forehead like I exhausted him. "Contrary to what you believe, I don't hate you, Darcie."

"Sure. Let's go with that." I rolled my eyes, rolling up the silverware.

"I'm trying to ask what's going on. No ulterior motives." I eyed him, assessing his sincerity. He did look like he was being honest, with no plans to dump a bucket of ice on me.

"Fine, but I doubt there's anything you can do. I had a friend from an, um, chat room that I've lost contact with. I don't know their real name or even where they live, and the server is down, so there's no way for me to get in touch with them. I just miss them and want them to know I'm okay too."

"Hmm, yeah, that sucks. Sorry."

"Man, I was hoping you were secretly a tech whiz and were going to tell me some simple solution and make me feel dumb."

"Sorry to bust your fantasy."

"Yeah, well, thanks anyway." I finished the rolling and moved on to the schedule when I felt his presence over me. I peeked over my shoulder, finding him closer.

"Can I help you?"

He opened his mouth, stopping before he said anything. His face was close to mine, and I watched as his eyes dropped down to my lips, licking his own. Damon glanced back up, his pupils more blown this time. He started to say something again when Buck walked in.

"Darcie, can we do the Cowboy Hustle tonight? I'm dressed to impress." We both looked over, finding Buck in a full cowboy getup. When he turned, I caught the assless chaps, and he shook his butt at us. Buck was the perfect counterpart to my crazy. I tried to swallow the sadness at the mention of Cowboy.

"Um, sure, but you're gonna have to put something on. You know the rules."

"Fine. I only did it to see you laugh anyway. You've been down lately."

"I'm good." I forced a smile and realized I needed to get out of this funk. I couldn't let it affect things.

"Your cute friend coming tonight? LJ?" he asked, wiggling his eyebrows at me.

"Get in line, lover boy." I turned back to the schedule and realized that Damon had moved away, his body heat no longer along my back. Had I envisioned that, or had he been about to kiss me?

When he called in sick the next night, he was officially back on my hate list, making me have to pull a double. I was going to need the world's largest coffee to make it to breakfast to meet Lennox.

A COUPLE MONTHS LATER

Hanging up the phone, I was glad that Lennox and her guys were safe. I couldn't believe that Thane had turned out to be a psycho stalker. I guess it showed people could pretend to be whoever they wanted.

Lennox told me she was staying in Bowling Green, KY to be closer to her family and help Slade with the opening of the new shop. Despite the crazy stalker, she'd gotten her happily ever after with her three guys. I was happy for my best friend, and thankful she was close, so I could visit her whenever I needed to get away.

But I missed her. We'd become soul sisters in such a short time, and now I felt lonely without her.

After the fallout with Cam Girls, Candi had shacked up with her sugar daddy and rarely went out anymore. I wasn't sure if she was embarrassed or just not interested in that lifestyle since she was all loved up.

In a way, I couldn't blame her, but I missed her friendship, too.

With both of them gone, I only had my job, which was becoming less and less fun.

"Damon, can I speak with you, please?" I asked, already hating this conversation. He looked at me, gritting his teeth, but followed.

Once he walked into the office, I closed the door and stayed standing. He glared at me, not saying a word. I sighed, not moving. He wasn't going to use his height to intimidate me.

"Do you know why I asked you back here?"

"Because you drew the short straw?" he asked.

"Sort of. I'm also the only one not scared of you. You've been here longer than any of us and we let you take the most leeway with everything. You call in at least once a week. You pass off your closing duties and never pick up extra shifts. You're grumpy most of the time, and if you weren't hot, I doubt you'd get any tips. You're a good bartender, but you have horrible customer service skills. Quite frankly, I'm not sure why you stay at this job that you clearly hate." I stared at him, my breathing heavy as I laid it all out. I found it was always better to be slightly angry with Damon, so he couldn't catch you off guard with his own.

He took a step forward, and I realized my mistake of staying against the door. I'd blocked his exit, but it also allowed him to trap me against it. Damon towered over me, bracing his hands against the door, glaring daggers at me.

"You know why I stay."

"No, I don't." I crossed my arms, pushing him a little away from me.

"Do you know why I call in? Why I can barely stand to be here some days but can't seem to stay away?"

"No, but I'd like to know. Maybe then we can find a solution."

His hand gripped my chin, tilting it up. "The only solution is this." His lips slammed down on mine, and it was a kiss to change the world. My body pressed into his, my hands threading through his hair, feeling the small hairs tickle the palm of my hand. He lifted me up, and I wrapped my legs around him as he continued to devour me against the door.

"Wait, you hate me. *We* hate each other."

"No, Darcie, I only hate myself for letting my brother get his hands on you first. I'm not boyfriend material, but I can't seem to quit thinking about you. I don't even need this job, but I stay because of you. It eats me up to see you going home with all of these losers every night instead of me, but I don't say anything, too scared I'd lost my chance all those years ago."

"You're an idiot."

I pulled him back to me, needing his lips on mine like I needed oxygen. His hands started to unbutton my shirt, and I grabbed at him, needing to feel his skin. His mouth began to plant hot, open-mouth kisses on my body, and I couldn't take it any longer. I dropped to the ground, pulling my shorts off in one go, unbuckling his belt. He turned me, pulling my head back to look at him.

"I don't do soft, sweetheart. I'm nothing like my brother."

"Good. Your bother was shit at fucking."

Damon smiled, and I realized it was one of the only full ones I'd ever seen. It caught me off guard, so when he slammed into me, I screamed, my eyes rolling back. His hand clamped down around my lips, and I bit into his fingers. He kept my head pulled back, maintaining eye contact as he pounded into me.

The Salvatore brothers didn't seem to like foreplay, but I suppose Damon and I had been teasing one another for years. The fact he slid in so smoothly, my wetness already dripping for him, was a testament to that fact.

"You're mine now, Darcie. Do you understand?"

I couldn't answer him, his cock too deep as he plunged in and out. Something felt wrong with agreeing, so I managed to only moan out my pleasure.

"Darcie?"

"No. I don't belong to anyone."

He stopped mid-thrust. "I'm not going to share you, Darcie. It's either me or nothing."

I blinked, trying to process what he said, and I realized the feeling I'd registered earlier.

"I'm sorry, Damon, but I can't promise you that. Why do I have to choose? My heart is capable of a lot of love."

His face screwed up, and he withdrew. "Don't tell me you want what your crazy little friend has? I saw her with those two guys on the dance floor."

I turned, not caring I was naked, planting my hands on my hips. "She actually has three boyfriends, and yeah, if I had the chance, I'd take it. Love doesn't have to be only one way. There are people in my life that have already claimed a piece of my heart. I might not ever see them again, but I can't tell you that I wouldn't want to be with them if they walked through that door right now, because I would."

Damon stared at me for a long moment, pulling his pants up and putting his shirt back on. I gathered my clothes, too, not wanting to be naked now that it was apparent this was stopping.

"I thought the whole slut thing was a phase, but I guess I was wrong. Don't worry about firing me. I quit."

He opened the door, slamming it shut, and I stood there staring, wondering what the hell had just happened.

A FEW MONTHS LATER

Dragging my feet, I tried to convince myself it was only a few more steps. The past few months had been miserable, and I didn't know what I was even doing here anymore. My job was a job. My friends were gone. And I didn't even want to hook up with anyone after the failed attempt with Damon. I needed a change. I just needed to figure out where. I'd even gone to the bank and cleaned out the safe deposit box in preparation. Something had kept holding me back from loading up my car and driving to wherever my car took me.

But I didn't think I could wait on whatever it was any longer. I needed a change of scenery.

Opening my apartment, a voice called out to me when I turned on the lights.

"Darcie."

I screamed, dropped my phone, and rushed to the man currently bleeding out in my kitchen. Seemed like change had just waltzed through my door.

Diary #14

Dear Mom,

I'm considering joining that convent. Or maybe I'll just go on vacation. I hear that's good for the soul. I've always wanted to travel more. Maybe I should. Nothing is holding me to Nashville. Not any more.

Love,

Darcie

Fifteen

DARCIE

"Holy Shit, Chase! What happened?" I rushed forward, grabbing some paper towels to press to his side.

"I'm good, Darcie. It's just a flesh wound. Bleeds more than it should." He groaned when I pressed the towel to him, and I rolled my eyes.

"Yeah, I'm not buying that. Start talking."

"I got into a little fight. It's no biggie."

"Uh-huh. So, you just happened to be in Nashville, about twelve hours from where you live, and found your way into my apartment, that you've never been to before, after a fight. Did I leave anything out?"

"That about covers it." He grinned, attempting to flirt even while injured.

Cursing under my breath, I placed his hand on

the spot I'd been pressing and stood walking to the sink to grab some water and the first aid kit. I looked him over as I set the things on the table, noticing some bruising around his eye. Whoever he'd gotten into it with had given him a black eye, too.

Thankfully, part of my training for MCD was first aid, so the steps quickly fell into place as I cleaned and dressed the wound. He was right; it wasn't deep, but I wasn't sure if butterfly bandages would be enough.

"I think you might need stitches."

"Nah, chicks dig scars."

"I'm more worried about you bleeding out, jackass."

"Ah, so you do care about me?"

Rolling my eyes, I stood and cleaned up all the items and placed them in the trash. Washing my hands, I scrubbed them for a good minute.

"Sit tight. I'll grab you something to wear."

He snorted, and I knew he wasn't going anywhere any time soon. Sighing, I changed my own clothes and found an oversized t-shirt I'd been given for a charity 5K I'd done last spring. Walking back into the kitchen, I helped him ease it over his head, trying not to smile at the sight of his handsome face in a pink tie-dyed shirt.

"Haha. I bet you're enjoying this."

"I am, a little. Though, I don't enjoy seeing you hurt. Gonna tell me now what's going on?"

"Nothing to tell. Quit your worrying, grandma."

"Fine, keep your secrets. You hungry?" I asked, walking over to the fridge and pulling out a pizza.

"I could eat."

Following the directions carefully, I preheated the oven and put the pizza on a pan, waiting for it to beep it was ready.

"Just add time," Chase said, watching me.

"Nope. I respect the directions. Things don't get burned if I follow them."

The oven beeped, and I set it in delicately, closing it. I put on the oven timer and then turned, crossing my arms to give Chase my death stare, hoping it would make him crack.

"You know, you're not really intimidating in a koala PJ-set, more cute than anything. It's the socks that really do it for me, though."

"Har dee har har. I'll have you know, I can force it out of you. I have ways."

"Oh, I'm sure you do, *Rose.*" He gave me a pointed look, and I stopped, frozen. Swallowing, I narrowed my eyes at him.

"How do you know that name?"

"Easy, I'm Dark Angel. I'm one of your biggest fans." The name made my insides freeze. He was a client that I'd talked to a lot, but had started to distance myself from when he'd gotten pushy. Something always felt off about it, and I guess now I knew why making fear spike even more.

"I'm still bummed you hadn't given me a private session, though. We could've finally had our moment."

Ice ran through my veins, and I hardened myself as I watched something in him flip. This was the Chase who'd assaulted me by the pool, not the one who'd seen the evidence of his father's rape running down my legs, giving me mercy. I had to tread carefully. This wasn't the Chase I'd been corresponding with for years.

"What do you want?" I asked, cutting to the chase.

"Always the smart one." He sat up, still clutching his side. "Your boy's in jail and is poised to get a deal soon. I want you to tell him not to."

"And why would I do that?" I asked, trying to hide the fact it was news to me that Maddox was in jail. It had been over a year since I'd seen or heard from him, so now I at least knew why.

"Because, if you don't, then I'll tell my father where you are."

"After all this time, why now? I thought we were friends, or at least had a kinship." Inside I was quivering, my whole body rattling with nerves. I didn't want to be on the run from Agonizer. Not now. I was finally settled, free of my past. I wouldn't let him take my healing from me. I was tired of men deciding my future for me.

He scoffed, rolling his eyes. His pretty face made me want to punch it and ugly it up a little more. He'd lured me into a false sense of security with his handsomeness. All along, he'd been the vile one, slithering in the grass, waiting until the right time to strike. He was worse than his father. Chase made you believe he was on your side and then pulled the rug out from under you when you were least expecting it. If he wasn't doing it to me, I'd be marveling at his genius.

"Because you've outgrown your purpose. I thought if I waited long enough, you'd come back to me. Even after tipping off that asshole back in Memphis that you were an easy lay, so you'd have to reach out to me, you didn't. I've been waiting all these years. When you started prostituting yourself out to the entire world, it was the last straw. I tried to make a connection with you, but even online, you were a cold, withholding bitch. So, it's time you were useful to me. I've outgrown this game, and I no longer want you since you've given yourself over to any man who pays you a compliment."

The air felt thin, and I stumbled back, grasping

hold of the counter. "Get out."

"Oh, I'm staying, Princess. I came for a reason. Thanks for patching me up, by the way. That was really kind of you."

"I told you not to call me that. If you don't get out, I'll call 911."

"Go ahead. I'll tell them your real name and that you're the daughter of one of Mississippi's notorious gang members and wanted in questioning for the murder of Bill Henshaw in Memphis. I'm sure they'd be really thankful to me for bringing them you."

I saw red, unable to think, the air around me constricting my lungs in a panic. I wouldn't go back to how I was. I wouldn't. Reaching down into the sink, my hand clasped down over the knife I'd used to cut the plastic over the pizza. Chase stared at me, his smug expression mocking.

He thought he'd won, but I was done with men telling me how I got to live my life. I was done with men trying to dictate it should be a certain way. Years of repressed trauma, along with all the healing and growth I'd done, surged forward, and I didn't even have to think as I plunged the knife into his chest, opening up the wound I'd just closed. Chase's eyes went wide as he stared at me in shock.

"The answer is fucking no." I pulled the knife out and took off running for the door, grabbing the go bag I always had ready. I clutched the knife in my hand, not caring how I looked as I bolted down the back stairs, my bare feet echoing off the concrete as I ran.

I had to go. I didn't want to, but I had to. For now, at least.

With shaking hands, I unlocked the car I'd never used and started it up. I'd taken my father's advice to heart this time and had my contingency plan ready.

I still wasn't great at driving four wheels, but nothing like the present to practice.

The further I got from the apartment, the better I felt. There was no way he could track me in this car. So, for now, I was safe. I avoided the cameras, and this car wasn't even registered in my name. I guess in some ways, I'd always known I'd have to run again. Thankfully, everything that meant something had been packed into the trunk in a secret compartment. My mom's belongings and the contents of the safe deposit box. If Maddox was in jail, his mission to save his sister must've failed. It was up to me now.

Gripping the steering wheel, I thought through my head where I could go, where it would be safe, and only one place came to mind.

Lennox. I had to get to Lennox.

Darcie's Story will continue in Beautiful Envy

Afterword

Thank you for reading Darcie's story. The words on the pages flew out of me and I knew I needed to get them down. I hope you enjoyed reading about her journey so far. She's a feisty one, and the guys that are coming into her life soon, they won't know what hit them.

Thank you to my alpha readers, Emma and Megan for being there to read through it with me and encourage me as I got her story down. Your enthusiasm as you read her story was everything.

Thank you to Kayla and Lindsay who always have time to read through my stories and give me valuable feedback. You girls are amazing.

Thanks to my husband for being there for me and giving me the space and time to write. I love you.

To you the reader, thank you as well for taking a chance on this story and diving into Darcie's world. I can't wait to see what is to come.

Also By Kris Butler

THE COUNCIL SERIES

(completed series)

Damaged Dreams

Shattered Secrets

Fractured Futures

Bosh Bells & Epic Fails

Council Boxset With Bonus

THE ORDER DUET (COUNCIL SPINOFF)

Stiletto Sins

Lipstick Lies

DARK CONFESSIONS

Dangerous Truths

Dangerous Lies

Dangerous Vows

Reckless (Cami's Novella)

Relentless (Nat's Novella)

Dangerous Love

TATTOOED HEARTS DUET

Tattooed Hearts Completed Duet

Riddled Deceit (Part 1)

Smudged Lines (Part 2)

Open Road

MUSIC CITY DIARIES

Beautiful Agony

Beautiful Envy

VACATION ROMCOM

Vibing

SINNERS FAIRYTALES

(standalone)

Pride

About the Author

Kris Butler writes under a pen name to have some separation from her everyday life. Never expecting to write a book, she was surprised when an author friend encouraged her to give it a try and how much she enjoyed it. Having an extensive background in mental health, Kris hopes to normalize mental health issues and the importance of talking about them with her characters and books. Kris is a southern girl at heart but lives with her husband and adorable furbaby somewhere in the Midwest. Kris is an avid fan of Reverse Harem and hopes to add a quirky and new perspective to the emerging genre. If you enjoyed her book, please consider leaving a review. You can contact her the following ways and follow Kris's journey as a new author on social media.